Gossip in a Library

Edmund Gosse

Contents

GOSSIP IN A LIBRARY

BY

Edmund Gosse

O blessed Letters, that combine in one All ages past, and make one live with all: By you we doe conferre with who are gone, And the dead-living unto councell call: By you th' unborne shall have communion Of what we feele, and what doth us befall.

SAM. DANIEL Musophilus. 1602.

INTRODUCTORY

It is curious to reflect that the library, in our customary sense, is quite a modern institution. Three hundred years ago there were no public libraries in Europe. The Ambrosian, at Milan, dates from 1608; the Bodleian, at Oxford, from 1612. To these Angelo Rocca added his in Rome, in 1620. But private collections of books always existed, and these were the haunts of learning, the little glimmering hearths over which knowledge spread her cold fingers, in the darkest ages of the world. To-day, although national and private munificence has increased the number of public libraries so widely that almost every reader is within reach of books, the private library still flourishes. There are men all through the civilised world to whom a book is a jewel--an individual possession of great price. I have been asked to gossip about my books, for I also am a bibliophile. But when I think of the great collections of fine books, of the libraries of the magnificent, I do not know whether I dare admit any stranger to glance at mine. The Mayor of Queenborough feels as though he were a very important personage till Royalty drives through his borough without noticing his scarf and his cocked hat; and then, for the first time, he observes how small the Queenborough town-hall is. But if one is to gossip about books, it is, perhaps, as well that one should have some limits. I will leave the masters of bibliography to sing of greater matters, and will launch upon no more daring voyage than one *autour de ma pauvre bibliotheque*.

I have heard that the late Mr. Edward Solly, a very pious and worshipful lover of books, under several examples of whose book-plate I have lately reverently placed my own, was so anxious to fly all outward noise that he built himself a library in his garden. I have been told that the books stood there in perfect order, with the rose-spray flapping at the window, and great Japanese vases exhaling such odours as most annoy an insect-nostril. The very bees would come to the window, and sniff, and boom indignantly away again. The silence there was perfect. It must have been in such a secluded library that Christian Mentzelius was at work when he heard the male book-worm flap his wings, and crow like a cock in calling to his mate. I feel sure that even Mentzelius, a very courageous writer, would hardly pretend that he could hear such a "shadow of all sound" elsewhere. That is the library I should like to have. In my sleep, "where dreams are multitude," I sometimes fancy that one day I shall have a library in a garden. The phrase seems to contain the whole felicity of man--"a library in a garden!" It sounds like having a castle in Spain, or a sheep-walk in Arcadia, and I suppose that merely to wish for it is to be what indignant journalists call "a faddling hedonist."

In the meanwhile, my books are scattered about in cases in different parts of a double sitting-room, where the cats carouse on one side, and the hurdy-gurdy man girds up his loins on the other. A friend of Boethius had a library lined with slabs of ivory and pale green marble. I like to think of that when I am jealous of Mr. Frederick Locker-Lampson, as the peasant thinks of the White Czar when his master's banqueting hall dazzles him. If I cannot have cabinets of ebony and cedar, I may just as well have plain deal, with common glass doors to keep the dust out. I detest your Persian apparatus.

It is a curious reflection, that the ordinary private person who collects objects of a modest luxury, has nothing about him so old as his books. If a wave of the rod made everything around him disappear that did not exist a century ago, he would suddenly find himself with one or two sticks of furniture, perhaps, but otherwise alone with his books. Let the work of another century pass, and certainly nothing but these little brown volumes would be left, so many caskets full of passion and tenderness, disappointed ambition, fruitless hope, self-torturing envy, conceit aware, in maddening lucid moments, of its own folly. I think if Mentzelius had been worth his salt, those ears of his, which heard the book-worm crow, might have caught the echo of a sigh from beneath many a pathetic vellum cover. There is something awful to me, of nights, and when I am alone, in thinking of all the souls imprisoned in the ancient books around me. Not one, I suppose, but was ushered into the world with pride and glee, with a flushed cheek and heightened pulse; not one enjoyed a career that in all points justified those ample hopes and flattering promises.

The outward and visible mark of the citizenship of the book-lover is his book-plate. There are many good bibliophiles who abide in the trenches, and never proclaim their loyalty by a book-plate. They are with us, but not of us; they lack the courage of their opinions; they collect with timidity or carelessness; they have no need for the morrow. Such a man is liable to great temptations. He is brought face to face with that enemy of his species, the borrower, and dares not speak with him in the gate. If he had a book-plate he would say, "Oh! certainly I will lend you this volume, if it has not my book-plate in it; of course, one makes a rule never to lend a book that has." He would say this, and feign to look inside the volume, knowing right well that this safeguard against the borrower is there already. To have a book-plate gives a collector great serenity and self-confidence. We have laboured in a far more conscientious spirit since we had ours than we did before. A learned poet, Lord De Tabley, wrote a fascinating volume on book-plates, some years ago, with copious illustrations. There is not, however, one specimen in his book which I would exchange for mine, the work and the gift of one of the most imaginative of American artists, the late Edwin A. Abbey. It represents a very fine gentleman of about 1610, walking in broad sunlight in a garden, reading a little book of verses. The name is coiled around him, with the motto, ***Gravis cantantibus umbra***. I will not presume to translate this tag of an eclogue, and I only venture to mention such an uninteresting matter, that my indulgent readers may have a more vivid notion of what I call my library. Mr. Abbey's fine art is there, always before me, to keep my ideal high.

To possess few books, and those not too rich and rare for daily use, has this advantage, that the possessor can make himself master of them all, can recollect their peculiarities, and often remind himself of their contents. The man that has two or three thousand books can be familiar with them all; he that has thirty thousand can hardly have a speaking acquaintance with more than a few. The more conscientious he is, the more he becomes like Lucian's amateur, who was so much occupied in rubbing the bindings of his books with sandal-wood and saffron, that he had no time left to study the contents. After all, with every due respect paid to "states" and editions and bindings and tall copies, the inside of the volume is really the essential part of it.

The excuses for collecting, however, are more than satire is ready to admit. The first edition represents the author's first thought; in it we read his words as he sent them out to the world in his first heat, with the type he chose, and with such peculiarities of form as he selected to do most justice to his creation. We often discover little individual points in a first edition, which never occur again. And if it be conceded that there is an advantage in reading a book in the form which the author originally designed for it, then all the other refinements of the collector become so many acts of respect paid to this first virgin apparition, touching and suitable homage of cleanness and fit adornment. It is only when this homage becomes mere eye-service, when a book radically unworthy of such dignity is too delicately cultivated, too richly bound, that a poor dilettantism comes in between the reader and what he reads. Indeed, the best of volumes may, in my estimation, be destroyed as a possession by a binding so sumptuous that no fingers dare to open it for perusal. To the feudal splendours of Mr. Cobden-Sanderson, a tenpenny book in a ten-pound binding, I say fie. Perhaps the ideal library, after all, is a small one, where the books are carefully selected and thoughtfully arranged in accordance with one central code of taste, and intended to be respectfully consulted at any moment by the master of their destinies. If fortune made me possessor of one book of excessive value, I should hasten to part with it. In a little working library, to hold a first quarto of **Hamlet**, would be like entertaining a reigning monarch in a small farmhouse at harvesting.

Much has of late been written, however, and pleasantly written, about the collecting and preserving of books. It is not my intention here to add to this department of modern literature. But I shall select from among my volumes some which seem less known in detail to modern readers than they should be, and I shall give brief "retrospective reviews" of these as though they were new discoveries. In other cases, where the personal history of a well-known book seems worth detaching from our critical estimate of it, that shall be the subject of my lucubration. Perhaps it may not be an unwelcome novelty to apply to old books the test we so familiarly apply to new ones. They will bear it well, for in their case there is no temptation to introduce any element of prejudice. Mr. Bludyer himself does not fly into a passion over a squat volume published two centuries ago, even when, as in the case of the first edition of Harrington's ***Oceana***, there is such a monstrous list of errata that the writer has to tell us, by way of excuse, that a spaniel has been "questing" among his papers.

These scarce and neglected books are full of interesting things. Voltaire never made a more unfortunate observation than when he said that rare books were worth nothing, since, if they were worth anything, they would not be rare. We know better nowadays; we know how much there is in them which may appeal to only one man here and there, and yet to him with a voice like a clarion. There are books that have lain silent for a century, and then have spoken with the trumpet of a prophecy. We shall disdain nothing; we shall have a little criticism, a little anecdote, a little bibliography; and our old book shall go back to the shelves before it has had time to be tedious in its babbling.

CAMDEN'S "BRITANNIA"

BRITAIN: ***or a chorographical description of the most flourishing King-domes, England, Scotland and Ireland, and the Ilands adioyning; out of the depth of Antiquitie: beautified with Mappes of the severall Shires of England; Written first in Latine by William Camden, Clarenceux K. of A. Translated newly into English by Philemon Holland. Londini, Impensis Georgii Bishop & Joannis Norton, M.DC.X***.

There is no more remarkable example of the difference between the readers of our light and hurrying age and those who obeyed "Eliza and our James," than the fact that the book we have before us at this moment, a folio of some eleven hundred pages, adorned, like a fighting elephant, with all the weightiest panoply of learning, was one of the most popular works of its time. It went through six editions, this vast antiquarian itinerary, before the natural demand of the vulgar released it from its

Latin austerity; and the title-page we have quoted is that of the earliest English edition, specially translated, under the author's eye, by Dr. Philemon Holland, a laborious schoolmaster of Coventry. Once open to the general public, although then at the close of its first quarter of a century, the **Britannia** flourished with a new lease of life, and continued to bloom, like a literary magnolia, all down the seventeenth century. It Is now as little read as other famous books of uncompromising size. The bookshelves of to-day are not fitted for the reception of these heroic folios, and if we want British antiquities now, we find them in terser form and more accurately, or at least more plausibly, annotated in the writings of later antiquaries. Giant Camden moulders at his cave's mouth, a huge and reverend form seldom disturbed by puny passers-by. But his once popular folio was the life work of a particularly interesting and human person; and without affecting to penetrate to the darkest corners of the cavern, it may be instructive to stand a little while on the threshold.

When this first English edition of the **Britannia** was published, Camden was one of the most famous of living English writers. For one man of position who had heard of Shakespeare, there would be twenty, at least, who were quite familiar with the claims of the Head-master of Westminster and Clarenceux King-of-Arms. Camden was in his sixtieth year, in 1610; he had enjoyed slow success, violent detraction, and final triumph. His health was poor, but he continued to write history, eager, as he says, to show that "though I have been a studious admirer of venerable antiquity, yet have I not been altogether an incurious spectator of modern occurrences." He stood easily first among the historians of his time; he was respected and adored by the Court and by the Universities, and that his fame might be completed by the chrism of detraction, his popularity was assured from year to year by the dropping fire of obloquy which the Papists scattered from their secret presses. It had not been without a struggle that Camden had attained this pinnacle; and the **Britannia** had been his alpenstock.

This first English edition has the special interest of representing Camden's last thoughts. It is nominally a translation of the sixth Latin edition, but it has a good deal of additional matter supplied to Philemon Holland by the author, whereas later English issues containing fresh material are believed to be so far spurious. The **Britannia** grew with the life of Camden. He tells us that it was when he was a young man of six-and-twenty, lately started on his professional career as second master in

Westminster School, that the famous Dutch geographer, Abraham Ortelius, "dealt earnestly with me that I would illustrate this isle of Britain." This was no light task to undertake in 1577. The authorities were few, and these in the highest degree occasional or fragmentary. It was not a question of compiling a collection of topographical antiquities. The whole process had to be gone through "from the egg."

As a youth at Oxford, Camden had turned all his best attention to this branch of study, and what the ancients had written about England was intimately known to him. Any one who looks at his book will see that the first 180 pages of the ***Britannia*** could be written by a scholar without stirring from his chair at Westminster. But when it came to the minute description of the counties there was nothing for it but personal travel; and accordingly Camden spent what holidays he could snatch from his labours as a schoolmaster in making a deliberate survey of the divisions of England. We possess some particulars of one of these journeys, that which occupied 1582, in which he started by Suffolk, through Yorkshire, and returned through Lancashire. He was a very rapid worker, he spared no pains, and in 1586, nine years after Ortelius set him going, his first draft was issued from the press. In later times, and when his accuracy had been cruelly impeached, he set forth his claims to attention with dignity. He said: "I have in no wise neglected such things as are most material to search and sift out the truth. I have attained to some skill of the most ancient British and Anglo-Saxon tongues; I have travelled over all England for the most part, I have conferred with most skilful observers in each county.... I have been diligent in the records of this realm. I have looked into most libraries, registers and memorials of churches, cities and corporations, I have pored upon many an old roll and evidence ... that the honour of verity might in no wise be impeached."

It was no slight task to undertake such a work on such a scale. And when the first Latin edition appeared, it was hailed as a first glory in the diadem of Elizabeth. Specialists in particular counties found that Camden knew more about their little circle than they themselves had taken all their lives to learn. Lombard, the great Kentish antiquary, said that he never knew Kent properly, till he read of it in the ***Britannia***. But Camden was not content to rest on his laurels. Still, year by year, he made his painful journeys through the length and breadth of the land, and still, as new editions were called forth, the book grew from octavo into folio. Suddenly, about twelve years after its first unchallenged appearance, there was issued, like a bolt out of the blue, a very nasty pamphlet, called ***Discovery of certain Errors Published in the much-commended Britannia***, which created a fine storm in the antiquarian teapot. This attack was the work of a man who would otherwise be forgotten, Ralph Brooke, the York Herald. He had formerly been an admirer of Camden's, his "humble friend," he called himself; but when Camden was promoted over his head to be Clarenceux King-of-Arms, it seemed to Ralph Brooke that it became his duty to denounce the too successful antiquary as a charlatan. He accordingly fired off the unpleasant little gun already mentioned, and, for the moment, he hit Camden rather hard.

The author of the ***Britannia***, to justify his new advancement, had introduced into a fresh edition of his book a good deal of information regarding the descent of barons and other noble families. This was York Herald's own subject, and he was able to convict Camden of a startling number of negligences, and what he calls "many gross mistakings." The worst part of it was that York Herald had privately pointed out these blunders to Camden, and that the latter had said it was too much trouble to alter them. This, at least, is what the enemy states in his attack, and if this be true, it can hardly be doubled that Camden had sailed too long in fair weather, or that he needed a squall to recall him to the duties of the helm. He answered Brooke, who replied with increased contemptuous tartness. It is admitted that Camden was indiscreet in his manner of reply, and that some genuine holes had been pricked in his heraldry. But the ***Britannia*** lay high out of the reach of fatal pedantic attack, and this little cloud over the reputation of the book passed entirely away, and is remembered now only as a curiosity of literature.

In the preface the author quaintly admits that "many have found a defect in this work that maps were not adjoined, which do allure the eyes by pleasant portraitures, ... yet my ability could not compass it." They must, then, have been added at the last by a generous afterthought, for this book is full of maps. The maritime ones are adorned with ships in full sail, and bold sea-monsters with curly tails; the inland ones are speckled with trees and spires and hillocks. In spite of these old-fashioned oddities, the maps are remarkably accurate. They are signed by John Norden and William Kip, the master map-makers of that reign. The book opens with an account of the first inhabitants of Britain, and their manners and customs; how the Romans fared, and what antiquities they left behind, with copious plates of Roman coins.

By degrees we come down, through Saxons and Normans, to that work which was peculiarly Camden's, the topographical antiquarianism. He begins with Cornwall, "that region which, according to the geographers, is the first of all Britain," and then proceeds to what he calls "Denshire" and we Devonshire, a county, as he remarks, "barbarous on either side."

With page 822 he finds himself at the end of his last English county, Northumberland, looking across the Tweed to Berwick, "the strongest hold in all Britain," where it is "no marvel that soldiers without other light do play here all night long at dice, considering the side light that the sunbeams cast all night long." This rather exaggerated statement is evidently that of a man accustomed to look upon Berwick as the northernmost point of his country, as we shall all do, no doubt, when Scotland has secured Home Rule. We are, therefore, not surprised to find Scotland added, in a kind of hurried appendix, in special honour to James I and VI. The introduction to the Scottish section is in a queer tone of banter; Camden knows little and cares less about the "commonwealth of the Scots," and "withall will lightly pass over it." In point of fact, he gets to Duncansby Head in fifty-two pages, and not without some considerable slips of information. Ireland interests him more, and he finally closes with a sheet of learned gossip about the outlying islands.

The scope of Camden's work did not give Philemon Holland much opportunity for spreading the wings of his style. Anxious to present Camden fairly, the translator is curiously uneven in manner, now stately, now slipshod, weaving melodious sentences, but forgetting to tie them up with a verb. He is commonly too busy with hard facts to be a Euphuist. But here is a pretty and ingenious passage about Cambridge, unusually popular in manner, and exceedingly handsome in the mouth of an Oxford man:

"On this side the bridge, where standeth the greater part by far of the City, you have a pleasant sight everywhere to the eye, what of fair streets orderly ranged, what of a number of churches, and of sixteen colleges, sacred mansions of the Muses, wherein a number of great learned men are maintained, and wherein the knowledge of the best arts, and the skill in tongues, so flourish, that they may rightly be counted the fountains of literature, religion and all knowledge whatsoever, who right sweetly bedew and sprinkle, with most wholesome waters, the gardens of the Church and Commonwealth through England. Nor is there wanting anything here, that a man may require in a most flourishing University, were it not that the air is somewhat unhealthful, arising as it doth out of a fenny ground hard by. And yet, peradventure, they that first founded a University in that place, allowed of Plato's judgment. For he, being of a very excellent and strong constitution of body, chose out the Academia, an unwholesome place of Attica, for to study in, and so the superfluous rankness of body which might overlay the mind, might be kept under by the dis-temperature of the place."

The poor scholars in the mouldering garrets of Clare, looking over waste land to the oozy Cam, no doubt wished that their foundress had been less Spartan. Very little of the domestic architecture that Camden admired in Cambridge is now left; and yet probably it and Oxford are the two places of all which he describes that it would give him least trouble to identify if he came to life again three hundred years after the first appearance of his famous *Britannia*.

A MIRROR FOR MAGISTRATES

A MIRROR FOR MAGISTRATES: *being a true Chronicle Historie of the untimely falles of such unfortunate Princes and men of note, as have happened since the first entrance of Brute into this Iland, untill this our latter Age. Newly enlarged with a last part, called* A WINTER NIGHTS VISION, *being an addition of such Tragedies, especially famous, as are exempted in the former Historie, with a Poem annexed, called* ENGLAND'S ELIZA. *At London. Imprinted by Felix Kyngston*, 1610.

This huge quarto of 875 pages, all in verse, is the final form, though far from the latest impression, of a poetical miscellany which had been swelling and spreading for nearly sixty years without ever losing its original character. We may obtain some imperfect notion of the *Mirror for Magistrates* if we imagine a composite poem planned by Sir Walter Scott, and contributed to by Wordsworth and Southey, being still issued, generation after generation, with additions by the youngest versifiers of to-day. The *Mirror for Magistrates* was conceived when Mary's protomartyrs were burning at Smithfield, and it was not finished until James I. had been on the throne seven years. From first to last, at least sixteen writers had a finger in this pie, and the youngest of them was not born when the eldest of them died.

It is commonly said, even by such exact critics as the late Dean Church, that the *Mirror for Magistrates* was planned by the most famous of the poets who took part in its execution, Thomas Sackville, Lord Buckhurst. If a very clever man is combined in any enterprise with people of less prominence, it is ten to one that he gets all the credit of the adventure. But the evidence on this point goes to prove that it was not until the work was well advanced that Sackville contributed to it at all. The inventor of the *Mirror for Magistrates* seems, rather, to have been George Ferrers, a prominent lawyer and politician, who was master of the King's Pastimes at the very close of Henry VIII.'s reign. Ferrers was ambitious to create a drama in England, and lacked only genius to be the British Aeschylus. The time was not ripe, but he was evidently very anxious to set the world tripping to his goatherd's pipe. He advertised for help in these designs, and the list of persons he wanted is an amusing one; he was willing to engage "a divine, a philosopher, an astronomer, a poet, a physician, an apothecary, a master of requests, a civilian, a clown, two gentlemen ushers, besides jugglers, tumblers, fools, friars, and such others," Fortune sent him, from Oxford, one William Baldwin, who was most of these things, especially divine and poet, and who became Ferrers' confidential factotum. The master and assistant-master of Pastimes were humming merrily on at their masques and triumphs, when, the King expired. Under Queen Mary, revels might not flourish, but the friendship between Ferrers and Baldwin did not cease. They planned a more doleful but more durable form of entertainment, and the *Mirror for Magistrates* was started. Those who claim for Sackville the main part of this invention, forget that he is not mentioned as a contributor till what was really the third edition, and that, when the first went to press, he was only eighteen years of age.

Ferrers well comprehended the taste of his age when he conceived the notion of a series of poems, in which famous kings and nobles should describe in their own persons the frailty and instability of worldly prosperity, even in those whom Fortune seems most highly to favour. One of the most popular books of the preceding century had been Lydgate's version of Boccaccio's poems on the calamities of illustrious men, a vast monody in nine books, all harping on that single chord of the universal mutability of fortune. Lydgate's *Fall of Princes* had, by the time that

Mary ascended the throne, existed in popular esteem for a hundred years. Its language and versification were now so antiquated as to be obsolete; it was time that princes should fall to a more modern measure.

The first edition of Baldwin and Ferrers' book went to press early in 1555, but of this edition only one or two fragments exist. It was "hindered by the Lord Chancellor that then was," Stephen Gardiner, and was entirely suppressed. The leaf in the British Museum is closely printed in double columns, and suggests that Baldwin and Ferrers meant to make a huge volume of it. The death of Mary removed the embargo, and before Elizabeth had been Queen for many months, the second (or genuine first) edition of the *Myrroure for Magistrates* made its appearance, a thin quarto, charmingly printed in two kinds of type. This contained twenty lives--Haslewood, the only critic who has described this edition, says *nineteen*, but he overlooked Ferrers' tale of "Humphrey, Duke of Gloucester"--and was the work, so Baldwin tells us, of seven persons besides himself.

The first story in the book, a story which finally appears at p. 276 of the edition before us, recounts the "Fall of Robert Tresilian, Chief Justice of England, and other of his fellows, for misconstruing the laws and expounding them to serve the Prince's affections, Anno 1388." The manner in which this story is presented is a good example of the mode adopted throughout the miscellany. The corrupt judge and his fellow-lawyers appear, as in a mirror, or like personages behind the illuminated sheet at the "Chat Noir," and lamentably recount their woes in chorus. The story of Tresilian was written by Ferrers, but the persons who speak it address his companion:

Baldwin, we beseech thee with our names to begin

--which support Baldwin's claim to be looked upon as the editor of the whole book. It is very dreary doggerel, it must be confessed, but no worse than most of the poetry indited in England at that uninspired moment in the national history. A short example--a flower culled from any of these promiscuous thickets--will suffice to give a general notion of the garden. Here is part of the lament of "The Lord Clifford":

Because my father Lord John Clifford died,
Slain at St. Alban's, in his prince's aid,

Against the Duke my heart for malice fired,
So that I could from wreck no way be stayed,
But, to avenge my father's death, assayed
All means I might the Duke of York to annoy,
And all his kin and friends for to destroy.
  This made me with my bloody dagger wound
His guiltless son, that never 'gainst me stored;
His father's body lying dead on ground
To pierce with spear, eke with my cruel sword
To part his neck, and with his head to board,
Invested with a royal paper crown,
From place to place to bear it up and down.
  But cruelty can never 'scape the scourge
Of shame, of horror, or of sudden death;
Repentance self that other sins may purge
Doth fly from this, so sore the soul it slayeth;
Despair dissolves the tyrant's bitter breath,
For sudden vengeance suddenly alights
On cruel deeds to quit their bloody spites.

The only contribution to this earliest form of the **Mirror** which is attributed to an eminent writer, is the "Edward IV" of Skelton, and this is one of the most tuneless of all. It reminds the ear of a whining ballad snuffled out in the street at night by some unhappy minstrel that has got no work to do. As Baldwin professes to quote it from memory, Skelton being then dead, perhaps its versification suffered in his hands.

This is not the place to enter minutely into the history of the building up of this curious book. The next edition, that of 1563, was enriched by Sackville's splendid "Induction" and the tale of "Buckingham," both of which are comparatively known so well, and have been so often reprinted separately, that I need not dwell upon them here. They occupy pp. 255-271 and 433-455 of the volume before us. In 1574 a very voluminous contributor to the constantly swelling tide of verse appears. Thomas Blener Hasset, a soldier on service in Guernsey Castle, thought that the magisterial ladies had been neglected, and proceeded in 1578 to sing the fall of princesses. It is needless to continue the roll of poets, but it is worth while to point out the remarkable fact that each new candidate held up the mirror to the magistrates so precisely in the manner of his predecessors, that it is difficult to distinguish Newton from Baldwin, or Churchyard from Niccols.

Richard Niccols, who is responsible for the collection in its final state, was a person of adventure, who had fought against Cadiz in the *Ark*, and understood the noble practice of the science of artillery. By the time it came down to him, in 1610, the *Mirror for Magistrates* had attained such a size that he was obliged to omit what had formed a pleasing portion of it, the prose dialogues which knit the tales in verse together, such pleasant familiar chatter between the poets as "Ferrers, said Baldwin, take you the chronicles and mark them as they come," and the like. It was a pity to lose all this, but Niccols had additions of his own verse to make; ten new legends entitled "A Winter Night's Vision," and a long eulogy upon Queen Elizabeth, "England's Eliza." He would have been more than human, if he had not considered all this far more valuable than the old prose babbling in black letter. This copy of mine is of the greatest rarity, for it contains two dedicatory sonnets by Richard Niccols, one addressed to Lady Elizabeth Clere and the other to the Earl of Nottingham, which seem to have been instantly suppressed, and are only known to exist in this and, I believe, one or two other examples of the book. These are, perhaps, worth reprinting for their curiosity. The first runs as follows:--

> My Muse, that whilom wail'd those Briton kings,
> Who unto her in vision did appear,
> Craves leave to strengthen her night-weathered wings
> In the warm sunshine of your golden Clere [clear];
> Where she, fair Lady, tuning her chaste lays
> Of England's Empress to her hymnic string
> For your affect, to hear that virgins praise,
> Makes choice of your chaste self to hear her sing,
> Whose royal worth, (true virtue's paragon,)
> Here made me dare to engrave your worthy name.
> In hope that unto you the same alone

Will so excuse me of presumptuous blame,

That graceful entertain my Muse may find

And even bear such grace in thankful mind.

The sonnet to the Earl of Nottingham, the famous admiral and quondam rival of Sir Walter Raleigh, is more interesting:--

    As once that dove (true honour's aged Lord),

Hovering with wearied wings about your ark,

When Cadiz towers did fall beneath your sword,

To rest herself did single out that bark,

So my meek Muse,--from all that conquering rout,

Conducted through the sea's wild wilderness

By your great self, to grave their names about

The Iberian pillars of Jove's Hercules,--

Most humbly craves your lordly lion's aid

'Gainst monster envy, while she tells her story

Of Britain's princes, and that royall maid

In whose chaste hymn her Clio sings your glory,

Which if, great Lord, you grant, my Muse shall frame

Mirrors most worthy your renowned name.

But apparently the "great Lord" would not grant permission, and so the sonnet had to be rigorously suppressed.

The **Mirror for Magistrates** has ceased to be more than a curiosity and a collector's rarity, but it once assumed a very ambitious function. It was a serious attempt to build up, as a cathedral is built by successive architects, a great national epic, the work of many hands. In a gloomy season of English history, in a violent age of tyranny, fanaticism, and legalised lawlessness, it endeavoured to present, to all whom it might concern, a solemn succession of discrowned tyrants and lawmakers smitten by the cruel laws they had made. Sometimes, in its bold and not very delicate way, the **Mirror for Magistrates** is impressive still from its lofty moral tone, its gloomy fatalism, and its contempt for temporary renown. As we read its sombre pages we see the wheel of fortune revolving; the same motion which makes the tiara glitter one moment at the summit, plunges it at the next into the pit of pain and oblivion. Steadily, uniformly, the unflinching poetasters grind out in their monotonous rime royal how "Thomas Wolsey fell into great disgrace," and how "Sir Anthony Woodville, Lord Rivers, was causeless imprisoned and cruelly wounded"; how "King Kimarus was devoured by wild beasts," and how "Sigeburt, for his wicked life, was thrust from his throne and miserably slain by a herdsman." It gives us a strange feeling of sympathy to realise that the immense popularity of this book must have been mainly due to the fact that it comforted the multitudes who groaned under a harsh and violent despotism to be told over and over again that cruel kings and unjust judges habitually came at last to a bad end.

A POET IN PRISON

THE SHEPHEARDS HUNTING: *being Certain Eglogues written during the time of the Authors Imprisonment in the Marshalsey. By George Wyther, Gentleman. London, printed by W. White for George Norton, and are to be sold at the signe of the red-Bull neere Temple-barre*. 1615.

If ever a man needed resuscitation in our antiquarian times it was George Wither. When most of the Jacobean poets sank into comfortable oblivion, which merely meant being laid with a piece of camphor in cotton-wool to keep fresh for us, Wither had the misfortune to be recollected. He became a byword of contempt, and the Age of Anne persistently called him Withers, a name, I believe, only possessed really by one distinguished person, Cleopatra Skewton's page-boy. Swift, in *The Battle of the Books*, brings in this poet as the meanest common trooper that he can mention in his modern army. Pope speaks of him with the utmost freedom as "wretched Withers." It is true that he lived too long and wrote too much--a great deal too much. Mr. Hazlitt gives the titles of more than one hundred of his publications, and some of them are wonderfully unattractive. I should not like to be shut up on a rainy day with his *Salt upon Salt*, which seems to have lost its savour, nor do I yearn to blow upon his *Tuba Pacifica*, although it was "disposed of rather for love than money." The truth is that good George Wither lost his poetry early, was an upright, honest, and patriotic man who unhappily developed into a scold, and got into the bad habit of pouring out "precautions," "cautional expressions," "prophetic phrensies," "epistles at random," "personal contributions to the national humiliation," "passages," "raptures," and "allarums," until he really became the greatest bore in Christendom. It was Charles Lamb who swept away this whole tedious structure of Wither's later writings and showed us what a lovely poet he was in his youth.

When the book before us was printed, George Wither was aged twenty-seven. He had just stepped gingerly out of the Marshalsea Prison, and his poems reveal an amusing mixture of protest against having been put there at all and deprecation of being put there again. Let no one waste the tear of sensibility over that shell of the Marshalsea Prison, which still, I believe, exists. The family of the Dorrits languished in quite another place from the original Marshalsea of Wither's time, although that also lay across the water in Southwark. It is said that the prison was used for the confinement of persons who had spoken lewdly of dignitaries about the Court. Wither, as we shall see, makes a great parade of telling us why he was imprisoned; but his language is obscure. Perhaps he was afraid to be explicit. In 1613 he had published a little volume of satires, called ***Abuses stript and whipt***. This had been very popular, running into six or seven editions within a short time, and some one in office, no doubt, had fitted on the fool's cap. Five years later the poor poet would have had a chance of being shipped straight off to Virginia, as a "debauched person"; as it was, the Marshalsea seems to have been tolerably unpleasant. We gather, however, that he enjoyed some alleviations. He could say, like Leigh Hunt, "the visits of my friends were the bright side of my captivity; I read verses without end, and wrote almost as many." The poems we have before us were written in the Marshalsea. The book itself is very tiny and pretty, with a sort of leafy trellis-work at the top and bottom of every page, almost suggesting a little posy of wild-flowers thrown through the iron bars of the poet's cage, and pressed between the pages of his manuscript. Nor is there any book of Wither's which breathes more deeply of the perfume of the fields than this which was written in the noisome seclusion of the Marshalsea.

Although the title-page assures us that these "eglogues" were written during the author's imprisonment, we may have a suspicion that the first three were composed just after his release. They are very distinct from the rest in form and character. To understand them we must remember that in 1614, just before the imprisonment,

Wither had taken a share with his bosom friend, William Browne, of the Inner Temple, in bringing out a little volume of pastorals, called *The Shepherd's Pipe*. Browne, a poet who deserves well of all Devonshire men, was two years younger than Wither, and had just begun to come before the public as the author of that charming, lazy, Virgilian poem of **Britannia's Pastorals**. There was something of Keats in Browne, an artist who let the world pass him by; something of Shelley in Wither, a prophet who longed to set his seal on human progress. In the **Shepherd's Pipe** Willy (William Browne) and Roget (Geo-t-r) had been the interlocutors, and Christopher Brooke, another rhyming friend, had written an eclogue under the name of Cutty. These personages reappear in *The Shepherd's Hunting*, and give us a glimpse of pleasant personal relations. In the first "eglogue," Willy comes to the Marshalsea one afternoon to condole with Roget, but finds him very cheerful. The prisoner poet assures his friend that

> This barren place yields somewhat to relieve,
> For I have found sufficient to content me,
> And more true bliss than ever freedom lent me;

and Willy goes away, when it is growing dark, rejoiced to find that "the cage doth some birds good." Next morning he returns and brings Cutty, or Cuddy, with him, for Cuddy has news to tell the prisoner that all England is taking an interest in him, and that this adversity has made him much more popular than he was before. But Willy and Cuddy are extremely anxious to know what it was that caused Roget's imprisonment, and at last he agrees to tell them. Hitherto the poem has been written in **ottava rima**, a form which is sufficiently uncommon in our early seventeenth-century poetry to demand special notice in this case. In a prose post-script to this book Wither tells us that the title, **The Shepherd's Hunting**, which he seems to feel needs explanation, is due to the stationer, or, as we should say now, to the publisher. But perhaps this was an afterthought, for in the account he gives to Willy and Cuddy he certainly suggests the title himself. He represents himself as the shepherd given up to the delights of hunting the human passions through the soul; the simile seems a little confused, because he represents these qualities not as the quarry, but as the hounds, and so the story of Actaeon is reversed; instead of the hounds pursuing their master, the master hunts his dogs. At all events, the result is that he "dips his staff in blood, and onwards leads his thunder to the wood," where he is ignominiously captured by his Majesty's gamekeeper. But the allegory hardly runs upon all-fours.

The next "eglogue" represents again another visit to the prisoner, and this time Willy and Cuddy bring Alexis with them; perhaps Alexis is John Davies, of Hereford, another contributor to *The Shepherd's Pipe*. Roget starts his allegory again, in the same mild, satiric manner he had adopted, to his hurt, in *Abuses stript and whipt*. Wither becomes quite delightful again, when cheerfulness breaks through this satirical philosophy, and when he tells us:

But though that all the world's delight forsake me, I have a Muse, and she shall music make me; Whose aery notes, in spite of closest cages, Shall give content to me and after ages.

They all felt certain of immortality, these cheerful poets of Elizabeth and James, and Prince Posterity has seen proper to admit the claim in more instances than might well have been expected.

But the delightful part of *The Shepherd's Hunting* has yet to come. With the fourth "eglogue" the caged bird begins to sing like a lark at Heaven's gate, and it is the prisoned man--who ought to be in doleful dumps--that rallies his free friend Browne on his low spirits. It is time, he says, to be merry:

Coridon, with his bold rout,
Hath already been about,
For the elder shepherds' dole,
And fetched in the summer pole;
Whilst the rest have built a bower
To defend them from a shower,
Sealed so close, with boughs all green,
Titan cannot pry between;
Now the dairy-wenches dream
Of their strawberries and cream,
And each doth herself advance,
To be taken in to dance.

What summer thoughts are these to come from a pale prisoner in the hot and putrid Marshalsea! They are either symptoms of acute nostalgia, or proofs of a cheerfulness that lifts their author above a mortal pitch. But Willy declines to join the Lady of the May at her high junketings; he also has troubles, and prefers to whisper them through Roget's iron bars. There are those who "my Music do contemn," who will none of the poetry of Master William Browne of the Inner Temple. It is useless for him to wrestle with brown shepherds for the

> Cups of turned maple-root,
> Whereupon the skilful man
> Hath engraved the Loves of Pan,

or contend for the "fine napkin wrought with blue," if those base clowns called critics are busy with his detraction. But Roget instructs him that Verse is its own high reward, that the songs of a true poet will naturally arise like the moon out of and beyond all racks of envious cloud, and that the last thing he should do is to despair. He rises to his own greatest and best work in this encouragement of a brother-poet, and no one who reads such noble verses as these dare question Wither's claim to a *fauteuil* in the Academy of Parnassus:

> If thy Verse do bravely tower
> As she makes wing, she gets power,
> Yet the higher she doth soar,
> She's affronted still the more;
> Till she to the highest hath past,
> Then she rests with Fame at last.
> Let nought therefore thee affright,
> But make forward in thy flight;
> For if I could match thy rhyme
> To the very stars I'd climb,
> There begin again, and fly
> Till I reached Eternity.

In the fifth "eglogue" Roget and Alexis compare notes about their early happiness in phrases of an odd commixture. The pastoral character of the poetry has to be carried out, and so we read of how Roget on a great occasion played a match at football, "having scarce twenty Satyrs on his side," against some of "the best tried Ruffians in the land." Great Pan presided at that match by the banks of Thames, and though the satyrs and their laureate leader were worsted, the moral victory, as people call it, remained with the latter. All this is an allegory; and indeed we walk in the very shadow of innuendo all through *The Shepherd's Hunting*.

The moral of the whole thing is that eternal ditty of tuneful youth: All for Verse and the World well lost. The enemy is around them on all sides, jailers of the Marshalsea and envious critics, the evil shepherds that preside over grates of steel and noisome beds of straw, but Youth has its mocking answer to all these:

> Let them disdain and fret till they are weary!
> We in ourselves have that shall make us merry;
> Which he that wants and had the power to know it,
> Would give his life that he might die a poet.

It was no small thing to be suffering for Apollo's sake in 1614. Shakespeare might hear of it at Stratford, and talk of the prisoner as he strolled with some friend on the banks of Avon. A greater than Shakespeare--as most men thought in those days--Ben Jonson himself, might talk the matter over "at those lyric feasts, Made at the Sun, The Dog, the triple Tun"; for had not he himself languished in a worse dungeon and under a heavier charge than Wither? To be seven-and-twenty, to be in trouble with the Government about one's verses, and to have other young poets, in a ferment of enthusiasm, clinging like swallows to the prison-bars--how delicious a torment! And to know that it will soon be over, and that the sweet, pure meadows lie just outside the reek of Southwark, that summer lingers still and that shepherds pipe and play, that Fame is sitting by her cheerful fountain with a garland for the weary head, and that lasses, "who more excell Than the sweet-voic'd Philomel," are ready to cluster round the Interesting captive, and lead him away in daisy-chains--what could be more consolatory! And we close the little dainty volume, with its delicate perfume of friendship and poetry and hope.

DEATH'S DUEL

DEATH'S DVELL; *or, A Consolation to the Soule, against the dying Life, and living Death of the Body. Delivered in a Sermon at White Hall, before the King's Maiesty, in the beginning of Lent,* 1630. *By that late learned and Reverend Divine, John Donne, Dr. in Divinity, & Deane of S. Pauls, London. Being his last Sermon, and called by his Maiesties houshold The Doctor's owne Funerall Sermon. London, Printed by Thomas Harper, for Richard Redmer and Benjamin Fisher, and are to be sold at the signe of the Talbot in Alders-gate street. MDCXXXII.*

The value of this tiny quarto with the enormous title depends entirely, so far as the collector is concerned, on whether or no it possesses the frontispiece. So many people, not having the fear of books before their eyes, have divorced the latter from the former, that a perfect copy of **Death's Duel** is quite a capture over which the young bibliophile may venture to glory; but let him not fancy that he has a prize if his copy does not possess the portrait-plate. One has but to glance for a moment at this frontispiece to see that there is here something very much out of the common. It is engraved in the best seventeenth-century style, and represents, apparently, the head and bust of a dead man wrapped in a winding-sheet. The eyes are shut, the mouth is drawn, and nothing was ever seen more ghastly.

Yet it is not really the picture of a dead man: it represents the result of one of the grimmest freaks that ever entered into a pious mind. In the early part of March 1630 (1631), the great Dr. Donne, Dean of St. Paul's, being desperately ill, and not likely to recover, called a wood-carver in to the Deanery, and ordered a small urn, just large enough to hold his feet, and a board as long as his body, to be produced. When these articles were ready, they were brought into his study, which was first warmed, and then the old man stripped off his clothes, wrapped himself in a winding-sheet which was open only so far as to reveal the face and beard, and then stood upright in the little wooden urn, supported by leaning against the board. His limbs were arranged like those of dead persons, and when his eyes had been closed, a painter was introduced into the room and desired to make a full-length and full-size picture of this terrific object, this solemn theatrical presentment of life in death. The frontispiece of **Death's Duel** gives a reproduction of the upper part of this picture. It was said to be a remarkably truthful portrait of the great poet and divine, and it certainly agrees in all its proportions with the accredited portrait of Donne as a young man.

It appears (for Walton's account is not precise) that it was after standing for this grim picture, but before its being finished, that the Dean preached his last sermon, that which is here printed. He had come up from Essex in great physical weakness in order not to miss his appointment to preach in his cathedral before the King on the first Friday in Lent. He entered the pulpit with so emaciated a frame and a face so pale and haggard, and spoke with a voice so faint and hollow, that at the end the King himself turned to one of his suite, and whispered, "The Dean has preached his own funeral sermon!" So, indeed, it proved to be; for he presently withdrew to his bed, and summoned his friends around to take a solemn farewell. He died very gradually after about a fortnight, his last words being, not in distress or anguish, but as it would seem in visionary rapture: "I were miserable if I might not die." All this fortnight and to the moment of his death, the terrible life-sized portrait of himself in his winding-sheet stood near his bedside, where it could be the "hourly object" of his attention. So one of the greatest Churchmen of the seventeenth century, and one of the greatest, if the most eccentric, of its lyrical poets passed away in the very pomp of death, on the 31st of March, 1631.

There was something eminently calculated to arrest and move the imagination in such an end as this, and people were eager to read the discourse which the "sacred authority" of his Majesty himself had styled the Dean's funeral sermon. It was therefore printed in 1632. As sermons of the period go it is not long, yet it takes a full hour to read it slowly aloud, and we may thus estimate the strain which it must have given to the worn-out voice and body of the Dean to deliver it. The present writer once heard a very eminent Churchman, who was also a great poet, preach his last sermon, at the age of ninety. This was the Danish bishop Grundtvig. In that case the effort of speaking, the extraction, as it seemed, of the sepulchral voice from the shrunken and ashen face, did not last more than ten minutes. But the English divines of the Jacobean age, like their Scottish brethren of to-day, were accustomed to stupendous efforts of endurance from their very diaconate.

The sermon is one of the most "creepy" fragments of theological literature it would be easy to find. It takes as its text the words from the sixty-eighth Psalm: "And unto God the Lord belong the issues of death." In long, stern sentences of sonorous magnificence, adorned with fine similes and gorgeous words, as the funeral trappings of a king might be with gold lace, the dying poet shrinks from no physical horror and no ghostly terror of the great crisis which he was himself to be the first to pass through. "That which we call life," he says, and our blood seems to turn chilly in our veins as we listen, "is but ***Hebdomada mortium***, a week of death, seven days, seven periods of our life spent in dying, a dying seven times over, and there is an end. Our birth dies in infancy, and our infancy dies in youth, and youth and rest die in age, and age also dies and determines all. Nor do all these, youth out of infancy, or age out of youth, arise so as a Phoenix out of the ashes of another Phoenix formerly dead, but as a wasp or a serpent out of a carrion or as a snake out of dung." We can comprehend how an audience composed of men and women whose ne'er-do-weel relatives went to the theatre to be stirred by such tragedies as those of Marston and Cyril Tourneur would themselves snatch a sacred pleasure from awful language of this kind in the pulpit. There is not much that we should call doctrine, no pensive or consolatory teaching, no appeal to souls in the modern sense. The effect aimed at is that of horror, of solemn preparation for the advent of death, as by one who fears, in the flutter of mortality, to lose some peculiarity of the skeleton, some jag of the vast crooked scythe of the spectre. The most ingenious of poets, the most subtle of divines, whose life had been spent in examining Man in the crucible of his own alchemist fancy, seems anxious to preserve to the very last his powers of unflinching spiritual observation. The Dean of St. Paul's, whose reputation for learned sanctity had scarcely sufficed to shelter him from scandal on the ground of his fantastic defence of suicide, was familiar with the idea of Death, and greeted him as a welcome old friend whose face he was glad to look on long and closely.

The leaves at the end of this little book are filled up with two copies of funeral verses on Dean Donne. These are unsigned, but we know from other sources to whom to attribute them. Each is by an eminent man. The first was written by Dr. Henry King, then the royal chaplain, and afterward Bishop of Chichester, to whom the Dean had left, besides a model in gold of the Synod of Dort, that painting of himself in the winding-sheet of which we have already spoken. This portrait Dr. King put into the hands of Nicholas Stone, the sculptor, who made a reproduction of it in white marble, with the little urn concealing the feet. This was placed in St. Paul's Cathedral, of which King was chief residentiary, and may still be seen in the present Cathedral King's elegy is very prosy in starting, but improves as it goes along, and is most ingenious throughout. These are the words in which he refers to the appearance of the dying preacher in the pulpit:

Thou (like the dying Swan) didst lately sing
Thy mournful dirge in audience of the King;
When pale looks, and weak accents of thy breath
Presented so to life that piece of death,
That it was feared and prophesied by all
Thou thither cam'st to preach thy funeral.

The other elegy is believed to have been written by a young man of twenty-one, who was modestly and enthusiastically seeking the company of the most famous London wits. This was Edward Hyde, thirty years later to become Earl of Clarendon, and finally to leave behind him manuscripts which should prove him the first great English historian. His verses here bespeak his good intention, but no facility in rhyming.

It was left for the riper disciples of the great divine to sing his funerals in more effective numbers. Of the crowd of poets who attended him with music to the grave, none expressed his merits in such excellent verses or with so much critical judgment as Thomas Carew, the king's sewer in ordinary. It is not so well known but that we quote some lines from it:

The fire
That fills with spirit and heat the Delphic choir,
Which, kindled first by thy Promethean breath,
Glow'd here awhile, lies quench'd now in thy death.
The Muses' garden, with pedantic weeds
O'erspread, was purg'd by thee, the lazy seeds
Of servile imitation thrown away,

And fresh invention planted; thou disdt pay
The debts of our penurious bankrupt age.

Whatsoever wrong
By ours was done the Greek or Latin tongue,
Thou hast redeem'd, and opened us a mine
Of rich and pregnant fancy, drawn a line
Of masculine expression, which, had good
Old Orpheus seen, or all the ancient brood
Our superstitious fools admire, and hold
Their lead more precious than thy burnish'd gold,
Thou hadst been their exchequer....
Let others carve the rest; it will suffice
I on thy grave this epitaph incise:--
Here lies a King, that ruled as he thought fit
The universal monarchy of wit;
Here lies two Flamens, and both these the best,--
Apollo's first, at last the True God's priest.

There was no full memoir of Dr. Donne until it was the privilege of the present writer, in 1900, to publish his Life and Letters in two substantial volumes. Since then, in 1912, his Poetical Works have been edited and sifted, with remarkable delicacy and judgment, by Professor Grierson. It is now, therefore, as easy as it can be expected ever to be to follow the career of this extraordinary man, with all its cold and hot fits, its rage of lyrical amativeness, its Roman passion, and the high and clouded austerity of its final Anglicanism. Donne is one of the most fascinating, in some ways one of the most inscrutable, figures in our literature, and we may contemplate him with instruction from his first wild escapade into the Azores down to his voluntary penitence in the pulpit and the winding-sheet.

GERARD'S HERBAL

THE HERBALL *or General Historie of Plantes. Gathered by John Gerarde, of London, Master in Chirurgerie. Very much enlarged and amended by Thomas Johnson, citizen and apothecarye of London. London, Printed by Adam Islip, Joice Norton, and Richard Whitakers. Anno* 1633.

The proverb says that a door must be either open or shut. The bibliophile is apt to think that a book should be either little or big. For my own part, I become more and more attached to "dumpy twelves"; but that does not preclude a certain discreet fondness for folios. If a man collects books, his library ought to contain a Herbal; and if he has but room for one, that should be the best. The luxurious and sufficient thing, I think, is to possess what booksellers call "the right edition of Gerard"; that is to say, the volume described at the head of this paper. There is no handsomer book to be found, none more stately or imposing, than this magnificent folio of sixteen hundred pages, with its close, elaborate letterpress, its innumerable plates, and John Payne's fine frontispiece in compartments, with Theophrastus and Dioscorides facing one another, and the author below them, holding in his right hand the new-found treasure of the potato plant.

This edition of 1633 is the final development of what had been a slow growth. The sixteenth century witnessed a great revival, almost a creation of the science of botany. People began to translate the great *Materia Medica* of the Greek physician, Dioscorides of Anazarba, and to comment upon it. The Germans were the first to append woodcuts to their botanical descriptions, and it is Otto Brunfelsius, in 1530, who has the credit of being the originator of such figures. In 1554 there was published the first great Herbal, that of Rembertus Dodonaeus, body-physician to the Emperor Maximilian II., who wrote in Dutch. An English translation of this, brought out in 1578, by Henry Lyte, was the earliest important Herbal in our language. Five years later, in 1583, a certain Dr. Priest translated all the botanical works of Dodonaeus, with much greater fulness than Lyte had done, and this volume was the germ of Gerard's far more famous production. John Gerard was a Cheshire man, born in 1545, who came up to London, and practised there as a surgeon.

According to his editor and continuator, Thomas Johnson, who speaks of Gerard with startling freedom, this excellent man was by no means well equipped for the task of compiling a great Herbal. He knew so little Latin, according to this too candid friend, that he imagined Leonard Fuchsius, who was a German contemporary of his own, to be one of the ancients. But Johnson is a little too zealous in magnifying his own office. He brings a worse accusation against Gerard, if I understand him rightly to charge him with using Dr. Priest's manuscript collections after his death, without giving that physician the credit of his labours. When Johnson made this accusation, Gerard had been dead twenty-six years. In any case it seems certain that Gerard's original ***Herbal***, which, beyond question, surpassed all its predecessors when it was printed in folio in 1597, was built up upon the ground-work of Priest's translation of Dodonaeus. Nearly forty years later, Thomas Johnson, himself a celebrated botanist, took up the book, and spared no pains to reissue it in perfect form. The result is the great volume before us, an elephant among books, the noblest of all the English Herbals. Johnson was seventy-two years of age when he got this gigantic work off his hands, and he lived eleven years longer to enjoy his legitimate success.

The great charm of this book at the present time consists in the copious woodcuts. Of these there are more than two thousand, each a careful and original study from the plant itself. In the course of two centuries and a half, with all the advance in appliances, we have not improved a whit on the original artist of Gerard's and Johnson's time. The drawings are all in strong outline, with very little attempt at shading, but the characteristics of each plant are given with a truth and a simplicity which are almost Japanese. In no case is this more extraordinary than in that of the orchids, or "satyrions," as they were called in the days of the old herbalist. Here, in a succession of little figures, each not more than six inches high, the peculiarity of every portion of a full-grown flowering specimen of each species is given with absolute perfection, without being slurred over on the one hand, or exaggerated on the other. For instance, the little variety called "ladies' tresses" [***Spiranthes***], which throws a spiral head of pale green blossoms out of dry pastures, appears here with small bells hanging on a twisted stem, as accurately as the best photograph could give it, although the process of woodcutting, as then practised in England, was very rude, and although almost all other English illustrations of the period are rough and inartistic. It is plain that in every instance the botanist himself drew the form, with which he was already intelligently familiar, on the block, with the living plant lying at his side.

The plan on which the herbalist lays out his letterpress is methodical in the extreme. He begins by describing his plant, then gives its habitat, then discusses its nomenclature, and ends with a medical account of its nature and virtues. It is, of course, to be expected that we should find the line old names of plants enshrined in Gerard's pages. For instance, he gives to the deadly nightshade the name, which now only lingers in a corner of Devonshire, the "dwale." As an instance of his style, I may quote a passage from what he has to say about the virtues, or rather vices, of this plant:

"Banish it from your gardens and the use of it also, being a plant so furious and deadly; for it bringeth such as have eaten thereof into a dead sleep wherein many have died, as hath been often seen and proved by experience both in England and elsewhere. But to give you an example hereof it shall not be amiss. It came to pass that three boys of Wisbeach, in the Isle of Ely, did eat of the pleasant and beautiful fruit hereof, two whereof died in less than eight hours after they had eaten of them. The third child had a quantity of honey and water mixed together given him to drink, causing him to vomit often. God blessed this means, and the child recovered. Banish, therefore, these pernicious plants out of your gardens, and all places near to your houses where children do resort."

Gerard has continually to stop his description that he may repeat to his readers some anecdote which he remembers. Now it is how "Master Cartwright, a gentleman of Gray's Inn, who was grievously wounded into the lungs," was cured with the herb called "Saracen's Compound," "and that, by God's permission, in short space." Now it is to tell us that he has found yellow archangel growing under a sequestered hedge "on the left hand as you go from the village of Hampstead, near London, to the church," or that "this amiable and pleasant kind of primrose" (a sort of oxlip) was first brought to light by Mr. Hesketh, "a diligent searcher after simples," in a Yorkshire wood. While the groundlings were crowding to see new plays by Shirley and Massinger, the editor of this volume was examining fresh varieties of auricula in "the gardens of Mr. Tradescant and Mr. Tuggie." It is wonderful how modern the latter statement sounds, and how ancient the former. But the garden seems the one spot on earth where history does not assert itself, and, no doubt, when Nero was fiddling over the blaze of Rome, there were florists counting the petals of rival roses at Paestum as peacefully and conscientiously as any gardeners of to-day.

The herbalist and his editor write from personal experience, and this gives them a great advantage in dealing with superstitions. If there was anything which people were certain about in the early part of the seventeenth century, it was that the mandrake only grew under a gallows, where the dead body of a man had fallen to pieces, and that when it was dug up it gave a great shriek, which was fatal to the nearest living thing. Gerard contemptuously rejects all these and other tales as "old wives' dreams." He and his servants have often digged up mandrakes, and are not only still alive, but listened in vain for the dreadful scream. It might be supposed that such a statement, from so eminent an authority, would settle the point, but we find Sir Thomas Browne, in the next generation, battling these identical popular errors in the pages of his ***Pseudodoxia Epidemica***. In the like manner, Gerard's botanical evidence seems to have been of no use in persuading the public that mistletoe was not generated out of birdlime dropped by thrushes into the boughs of trees, or that its berries were not desperately poisonous. To observe and state the truth is not enough. The ears of those to whom it is proclaimed must be ready to accept it.

Our good herbalist, however, cannot get through his sixteen hundred accurate and solemn pages without one slip. After accompanying him dutifully so far, we double up with uncontrollable laughter on p. 1587, for here begins the chapter which treats "of the Goose Tree, Barnacle Tree, or the Tree bearing Geese." But even here the habit of genuine observation clings to him. The picture represents a group of stalked barnacles--those shrimps fixed by their antennae, which modern science, I believe, calls ***Lepas anatifera***; by the side of these stands a little goose, and the suggestion of course is that the latter has slipped out of the former, although the draughtsman has been far too conscientious to represent the occurrence. Yet the letterpress is confident that in the north parts of Scotland there are trees on which grow white shells, which ripen, and then, opening, drop little living geese into the waves below. Gerard himself avers that from Guernsey and Jersey he brought home with him to London shells, like limpets, containing little feathery objects, "which, ***no doubt***, were the fowls called Barnacles." It is almost needless to say that these objects really were the plumose and flexible ***cirri*** which the barnacles throw out to catch their food with, and which lie, like a tiny feather-brush, just within the valves of the shell, when the creature is dead. Gerard was plainly unable to refuse credence to the mass of evidence which presented itself to him on this subject, yet he closes with a hint that this seems rather a "fabulous breed" of geese.

With the Barnacle Goose Tree the Herbal proper closes, in these quaint

words:

"And thus having, through God's assistance, discoursed somewhat at large of grasses, herbs, shrubs, trees and mosses, and certain excrescences of the earth, with other things moe, incident to the history thereof, we conclude, and end our present volume with this wonder of England. For the which God's name be ever honoured and praised."

And so, at last, the Goose Tree receives the highest sanction.

PHARAMOND

PHARAMOND; or, The History of France. A New Romance. In four parts. Written originally in French, by the Author of Cassandra and Cleopatra: and now elegantly rendered into English. London: Printed by Ja: Cottrell for Samuel Speed, at the Rain-Bow in Fleetstreet, near the Inner Temple-Gate. (Folio.) 1662.

There is no better instance of the fact that books will not live by good works alone than is offered by the utterly neglected heroic novels of the seventeenth century. At the opening of the reign of Louis XIV. in France, several writers, in the general dearth of prose fiction, began to supply the public in Paris with a series of long romances, which for at least a generation absorbed the attention of the ladies and reigned unopposed in every boudoir. I wonder whether my lady readers have ever attempted to realise how their sisters of two hundred years ago spent their time? In an English country-house of 1650, there were no magazines, no newspapers, no lawn tennis or croquet, no afternoon-teas or glee-concerts, no mothers' meetings or zenana missions, no free social intercourse with neighbours, none of the thousand and one agreeable diversions with which the life of a modern girl is diversified. On the other hand, the ladies of the house had their needlework to attend to, they had to "stitch in a clout," as it was called; they had to attend to the duties of a house-keeper, and, when the sun shone, they tended the garden. Perhaps they rode or drove, in a stately fashion. But through long hours they sat over their embroidery frames or mended the solemn old tapestries which lined their walls, and during these sedate performances they required a long-winded, polite, unexciting, stately book that might be read aloud by turns. The heroic novel, as provided by Gombre-

ville, Calprenede, and Mlle. de Scudery supplied this want to perfection.

The sentiments in these novels were of the most elevated class, and tedious as they seem nowadays to us, it was the sentiments, almost more than the action, which fascinated contemporary opinion. Madame de Sevigne herself, the brightest and wittiest of women, confessed herself to be a fly in the spider's web of their attractions. "The beauty of the sentiments," she writes, "the violence of the passions, the grandeur of the events, and the miraculous success of their redoubtable swords, all draw me on as though I were still a little girl." In these modern days of success, we may still start to learn that the Parisian publisher of *Le Grand Cyrus* made 100,000 crowns by that work, from the appearance of its first volume in 1649 to its close in 1653. The qualities so admirably summed up by Madame de Sevigne were those which appealed most directly to public feeling in France. There really were heroes in that day, the age of chivalric passions had not passed, great loves, great hates, great emotions of all kinds, were conceivable and within personal experience. When La Rochefoucauld wrote to Madame de Longueville the famous lines which may be thus translated:

> To win that wonder of the world,
> A smile from her bright eyes,
> I fought my King, and would have hurled
> The gods out of their skies,

he was breathing the very atmosphere of the heroic novels. Their extraordinary artificial elevation of tone was partly the spirit of the age; it was also partly founded on a new literary ideal, the tone of Greek romance. No book had been read in France with greater avidity than the sixteenth-century translation of the old novel *Heliodorus*; and in the *Polexandres* and *Clelies* we see what this Greek spirit of romance could blossom into when grafted upon the stock of Louis XIV.

The vogue of these heroic novels in England has been misstated, for the whole subject has but met with neglect from successive historians of literature. It has been asserted that they were not read in England until after the Restoration. Nothing is further from the truth. Charles I. read *Cassandra* in prison, while we find Dorothy Osborne, in her exquisite letters to Sir William Temple, assiduously study-

ing one heroic novel after another through the central years of Cromwell's rule. She reads *Le Grand Cyrus* while she has the ague; she desires Temple to tell her "which **amant** you have most compassion for, when you have read what each one says for himself." She and the King read them in the original, but soon there arrived English translations and imitations. These began to appear a good deal sooner than bibliographers have been prepared to admit. Of the *Astree* of D'Urfe--which, however, is properly a link between the *Arcadia* of Sidney and the genuine heroic novel--there was an English version as early as 1620. But, of the real thing, the first importation was *Polexandre*, in 1647, followed by *Cassandra* and *Ibrahim* in 1652, *Artamenes* in 1653, *Cleopatra* in 1654-8, and *Clelie* in 1655, all, it will be observed, published in England before the close of the Commonwealth.

Dorothy Osborne, who had studied the French originals, turned up her nose at these translations. She says that they were "so disguised that I, who am their old acquaintance, hardly knew them." They had, moreover, changed their form. In France they had come out in an infinite number of small, manageable tomes. For instance, Calprenede published his *Cleopatre* in twenty-three volumes; but the English *Cleopatra* is all contained in one monstrous elephant folio. *Artamenes*, the English translation of *Le Grand Cyrus*, is worse still, for it is comprised in five such folios. Many of the originals were translated over and over again, so popular were they; and as the heroic novels of any eminence in France were limited in number, it would be easy, by patiently hunting the translations up in old libraries, to make a pretty complete list of them. The principal heroic novels were eight in all; of these there is but one, the *Almahide* of Mlle, de Scudery, which we have not already mentioned, and the original publication of the whole school is confined within less than thirty years.

The best master in a bad class of lumbering and tiresome fiction was the author of the book which is the text of this chapter. La Calprenede, whose full name was nothing less than Gautier de Costes de la Calprenede, was a Gascon gentleman of the Guards, of whose personal history the most notorious fact is that he had the temerity to marry a woman who had already buried five husbands. Some historians relate that she proceeded to poison number six, but this does not appear to be certain, while it does appear that Calprenede lived in the married state for fifteen years, a longer respite than the antecedents of madame gave him any right to anticipate. He made a great fame with his two huge Roman novels, *Cassandra* and *Cleopatra*, and then, some years later, he produced a third, *Pharamond* which was taken out of early French history. The translator, in the version before us, says of this book that it "is not a romance, but a history adorned with some excellent flourishes of language and loves, in which you may delightfully trace the author's learned pen through all those historians who wrote of the times he treats of." In other words, while Gombreville--with his King of the Canaries, and his Vanishing Islands, and his necromancers, and his dragons--canters through pure fairyland, and while Mlle. de Scudery elaborately builds up a romantic picture of her own times (in *Clelie*, for instance, where the three hundred and seventy several characters introduced are said to be all acquaintances of the author), Calprenede attempted to produce something like a proper historical novel, introducing invention, but embroidering it upon some sort of genuine framework of fact.

To describe the plot of *Pharamond*, or of any other heroic novel, would be a desperate task. The great number of personages introduced in pairs, the intrigues of each couple forming a separate thread wound into the complex web of the plot, is alone enough to make any following of the story a great difficulty. On the fly-leaf of a copy of *Cleopatra* which lies before me, some dear lady of the seventeenth century has very conscientiously written out "a list of the Pairs of Lovers," and there are thirteen pairs. *Pharamond* begins almost in the same manner as a novel by the late Mr. G.P.R. James might. When the book opens we discover the amorous Marcomine and the valiant Genebaud sallying forth along the bank of a river on two beautiful horses of the best jennet-race. Throughout the book all the men are valiant, all the ladies are passionate and chaste. The heroes enter the lists covered with rubies, loosely embroidered over surcoats of gold and silk tissue; their heads "shine with gold, enamel and precious stones, with the hinder part covered with an hundred plumes of different colours." They are mounted upon horses "whose whiteness might outvie the purest snow upon the frozen Alps." They pierce into woodland dells, where they by chance discover renowned princesses, nonpareils of beauty, in imminent danger, and release them. They attack hordes of deadly pirates, and scatter their bodies along the shore; and yet, for all their warlike fire and force, they are as gentle as marmozets in a lady's boudoir. They are especially admirable in the putting forth of sentiments, in glozing over a subtle difficulty in love, in tying a knot of silk or fastening a lock of hair to their bonnet. They will steal into a cabinet so softly that a lady who is seated there, in a reverie, will not perceive them; they are so adroit that they will seize a paper on which she has sketched a couplet, will complete it, pass away, and she not know whence the poetical miracle has come. In valour, in courtesy, in magnificence they have no rival, just as the ladies whom they court are unique in beauty, in purity, in passion, and in self-denial. Sometimes they correspond at immense length; in *Pharamond* the letters which pass between the Princess Hunnimonde and Prince Balamir would form a small volume by themselves, an easy introduction to the art of polite letter-writing. Mlle. de Scudery actually perceived this, and published a collection of model correspondence which was culled bodily from the huge store-house of her own romances, from *Le Grand Cyrus* and *Clelie*. These interchanges of letters were kept up by the severity of the heroines. It was not thought proper that the lady should yield her hand until the gentleman had exhausted the resources of language, and had spent years of amorous labour on her conquest. When Roger Boyle, in 1654, published his novel of *Parthenissa*, in four volumes, Dorothy Osborne objected to the ease with which the hero succeeded; she complains "the ladies are all so kind they make no sport."

This particular 1662 translation of *Pharamond* appears to be very rare, if not unique. At all events I find it in none of the bibliographies, nor has the British Museum Library a copy of it. The preface is signed J.D., and the version is probably therefore from the pen of John Davies, who helped Loveday to finish his enormous translation of *Cleopatra* in 1665. In 1677 there came out another version of *Pharamond*, by John Phillips, and this is common enough. Some day, perhaps, these elephantine old romances may come into fashion again, and we may obtain a precise list of them. At present no corner of our literary history is more thoroughly neglected.[1]

[Note 1: Since this was written, a French critic of eminence, M. Jusserand, has made (in *The English Novel in the Time of Shakespeare*, 1890) a delightful contribution to this portion of our literary history. The earlier part of the last chapter of that volume may be recommended to all readers curious about the vogue of the heroic novel. But M. Jusserand does not happen to mention *Pharamond*, nor to cover the exact ground of my little study.]

A VOLUME OF OLD PLAYS

In his **Ballad of the Book-Hunter**, Andrew Lang describes how, in breeches baggy at the knees, the bibliophile hunts in all weathers:

No dismal stall escapes his eye;
He turns o'er tomes of low degrees;
There soiled romanticists may lie,
Or Restoration comedies.

That speaks straight to my heart; for of all my weaknesses the weakest is that weakness of mine for Restoration plays. From 1660 down to 1710 nothing in dramatic form comes amiss, and I have great schemes, like the boards on which people play the game of solitaire, in which space is left for every drama needed to make this portion of my library complete. It is scarcely literature, I confess; it is a sport, a long game which I shall probably be still playing at, with three mouldy old tragedies and one opera yet needed to complete my set, when the Reaper comes to carry me where there is no amassing nor collecting. It would hardly be credited how much pleasure I have drained out of these dramas since I began to collect them judiciously in my still callow youth. I admit only first editions; but that is not so rigorous as it sounds, since at least half of the poor old things never went into a second.

As long as it is Congreve and Dryden and Otway, of course it is literature, and of a very high order; even Shadwell and Mrs. Behn and Southerne are literature; Settle and Ravenscroft may pass as legitimate literary curiosity. But there are depths below this where there is no excuse but sheer collectaneomania. Plays by people who never got into any schedule of English letters that ever was planned, dramatic nonentities, stage innocents massacred in their cradles, if only they were published in quarto I find room for them. I am not quite so pleased to get these anonymities, I must confess, as I am to get a clean, tall **editio princeps** of *The Orphan* or of *Love for Love*. But I neither reject nor despise them; each of them counts one; each serves to fill a place on my solitaire board, each hurries on that dreadful possible time coming when my collection shall be complete, and I shall have nothing to do but break my collecting rod and bury it fathoms deep.

A volume has just come in which happens to have nothing in it but those forgotten plays, whose very names are unknown to the historians of literature. First comes *The Roman Empress*, by William Joyner, printed in 1671. Joyner was an Oxford man, a fellow of Magdalen College. The little that has been recorded about him makes one wish to know more. He became persuaded of the truth of the Catholic faith, and made a voluntary resignation of his Oxford fellowship. He had to do something, and so he wrote this tragedy, which he dedicated to Sir Charles Sedley, the poet, and got acted at the Theatre Royal. The cast contains two good actors' names, Mohun and Kynaston, and it seems that it enjoyed a considerable success. But doubtless the stage was too rough a field for the gentle Oxford scholar. He retired into a sequestered country village, where he lingered on till 1706, when he was nearly ninety. But Joyner was none of the worst of poets. Here is a fragment of *The Royal Empress*, which is by no means despicably versed:

O thou bright, glorious morning,
Thou Oriental spring-time of the day,
Who with thy mixed vermilion colours paintest
The sky, these hills and plains! thou dost return
In thy accustom'd manner, but with thee
Shall ne'er return my wonted happiness.

Through his Roman tragedy there runs a pensive vein of sadness, as though the poet were thinking less of his Aurelia and his Valentius than of the lost common-room and the arcades of Magdalen to be no more revisited.

Our next play is a worse one, but much more pretentious. It is the *Usurper*, of 1668, the first of four dramas published by the Hon. Edward Howard, one of Dryden's aristocratic brothers-in-law. Edward Howard is memorable for a couplet constantly quoted from his epic poem of *The British Princes*:

    A vest as admired Vortiger had on,   Which from a naked Pict his grandsire won.

Poor Howard has received the laughter of generations for representing Vortiger's grandsire as thus having stripped one who was bare already. But this is the wickedness of some ancient wag, perhaps of Dryden himself, who loved to laugh at his brother-in-law. At all events, the first (and, I suppose, only) edition of ***The British Princes*** is before me at this moment, and the second of these lines certainly runs:

Which from this island's foes his grandsire won.

Thus do the critics, leaping one after another, like so many sheep, follow the same wrong track, in this case for a couple of centuries. The ***Usurper*** is a tragedy, in which a Parasite, "a most perfidious villain," plays a mysterious part. He is led off to be hanged at last, much to the reader's satisfaction, who murmurs, in the words of R.L. Stevenson, "There's an end of that."

But though the ***Usurper*** is dull, we reach a lower depth and muddier lees of wit in the ***Carnival***, a comedy by Major Thomas Porter, of 1664. It is odd, however, that the very worst production, if it be more than two hundred years old, is sure to contain some little thing interesting to a modern student. The ***Carnival*** has one such peculiarity. Whenever any of the characters is left alone on the stage, he begins to soliloquise in the stanza of Gray's ***Churchyard Elegy***. This is a very quaint innovation, and one which possibly occurred to brave Major Porter in one of the marches and counter-marches of the Civil War.

But the man who perseveres is always rewarded, and the fourth play in our volume really repays us for pushing on so far. Here is a piece of wild and ghostly poetry that is well worth digging out of the Duke of Newcastle's ***Humorous Lovers***:

At curfew-time, and at the dead of night,
I will appear, thy conscious soul to fright,
Make signs, and beckon thee my ghost to follow
To sadder groves, and churchyards, where we'll hollo
To darker caves and solitary woods,
To fatal whirlpools and consuming floods;
I'll tempt thee to pass by the unlucky ewe,
Blasted with cursed droppings of mildew;
Under an oak, that ne'er bore leaf, my moans
Shall there be told thee by the mandrake's groans;

The winds shall sighing tell thy cruelty,
And how thy want of love did murder me;
And when the cock shall crow, and day grow near,
Then in a flash of fire I'll disappear.

But I cannot persuade myself that his Grace of Newcastle wrote those lines himself. Published in 1677, they were as much of a portent as a man in trunk hose and a slashed doublet. The Duke had died a month or two before the play was published; he had grown to be, in extreme old age, the most venerable figure of the Restoration, and it is possible that the ***Humorous Lovers*** may have been a relic of his Jacobean youth. He might very well have written it, so old was he, in Shakespeare's lifetime. But the Duke of Newcastle was never a very skilful poet, and it is known that he paid James Shirley to help him with his plays. I feel convinced that if all men had their own, the invocation I have just quoted would fly back into the works of Shirley, and so, no doubt, would the following quaintest bit of conceited fancy. It is part of a fantastical feast which Boldman promises to the Widow of his heart:

The twinkling stars shall to our wish
Make a grand salad in a dish;
Snow for our sugar shall not fail,
Fine candied ice, comfits of hail;
For oranges, gilt clouds will squeeze;
The Milky Way we'll turn to cheese;
Sunbeams we'll catch, shall stand in place
Of hotter ginger, nutmegs, mace;
Sun-setting clouds for roses sweet,
And violet skies strewed for our feet;
The spheres shall for our music play,
While spirits dance the time away.

This is extravagant enough, but surely very picturesque. I seem to see the supper-room of some Elizabethan castle after an elaborate royal masque. The Duchess, who has been dancing, richly attired in sky-coloured silk, with gilt wings on her shoulders, is attended to the refreshments by the florid Duke, personating the river Thamesis, with a robe of cloth of silver around him. It seems the sort of thing a poet so habited might be expected to say between a galliard and a coranto.

At first sight we seem to have reached a really good rhetorical play when we arrive at Bancroft's tragedy of *Sertorius*, published in 1679, and so it would be if Dryden and Lee had never written. But its seeming excellence is greatly lessened when we recollect that *All for Love* and *Mithridates*, two great poems which are almost good plays, appeared in 1678, and inspired our poor imitative Bancroft. *Sertorius* is written in smooth and well-sustained blank verse, which is, however, nowhere quite good enough to be quoted. I suspect that John Bancroft was a very interesting man. He was a surgeon, and his practice lay particularly In the theatrical and literary world. He acquired, it is said, from his patients "a passion for the Muses," and an inclination to follow in the steps of those whom he cured or killed. The dramatist Ravenscroft wrote an epilogue to *Sertorius*, in which he says that--

> Our Poet to learned critics does submit,
>
> But scorns those little vermin of the pit,
>
> Who noise and nonsense vent instead of wit,

and no doubt Bancroft had aims more professional than those of the professional playwrights themselves. He wrote three plays, and lived until 1696. One fancies the discreet and fervent poet-surgeon, laden with his secrets and his confidences. Why did he not write memoirs, and tell us what it was that drove Nat Lee mad, and how Otway really died, and what Dryden's habits were? Why did he not purvey magnificent indiscretions whispered under the great periwig of Wycherley, or repeat that splendid story about Etheredge and my Lord Mulgrave? Alas! we would have given a wilderness of *Sertoriuses* for such a series of memoirs.

The volume of plays is not exhausted. Here is Weston's *Amazon Queen*, of 1667, written in pompous rhymed heroics; here is *The Fortune Hunters*, a comedy of 1689, the only play of that brave fellow, James Carlile, who, being brought up an actor, preferred "to *be* rather than to *personate* a hero," and died in gallant fight for William of Orange, at the battle of Aughrim; here is *Mr. Anthony*, a comedy written by the Right Honourable the Earl of Orrery, and printed in 1690, a piece never republished among the Earl's works, and therefore of some special interest. But I am sure my reader is exhausted, even if the volume is not, and I spare him any further examination of these obscure dramas, lest he should say, as Peter Pindar did of Dr. Johnson, that I

Set wheels on wheels in motion--such a clatter!

To force up one poor nipperkin of water;

Bid ocean labour with tremendous roar

To heave a cockle-shell upon the shore.

I will close, therefore, with one suggestion to the special student of comparative literature--namely, that it is sometimes in the minor writings of an age, where the bias of personal genius is not strongly felt, that the general phenomena of the time are most clearly observed. *The Amazon Queen* is in rhymed verse, because in 1667 this was the fashionable form for dramatic poetry; *Sertorius* is in regular and somewhat restrained blank verse, because in 1679 the fashion had once more chopped round. What in Dryden or Otway might be the force of originality may be safely taken as the drift of the age in these imitative and floating nonentities.

A CENSOR OF POETS

The Lives of The Most Famous English Poets, *or the Honour of Parnassus; in a Brief Essay of the Works and Writings of above Two Hundred of them, from the Time of K. William the Conqueror, to the Reign of His Present Majesty King James II. Written by William Winstanley. Licensed June 16, 1686. London, Printed by H. Clark, for Samuel Manship at the Sign of the Black Bull in Cornhil,* 1687.

A maxim which it would be well for ambitious critics to chalk up on the walls of their workshops is this: never mind whom you praise, but be very careful whom you blame. Most critical reputations have struck on the reef of some poet or novelist whom the great censor, in his proud old age, has thought he might disdain with impunity. Who recollects the admirable treatises of John Dennis, acute, learned, sympathetic? To us he is merely the sore old bear, who was too stupid to perceive the genius of Pope. The grace and discrimination lavished by Francis Jeffrey over a thousand pages, weigh like a feather beside one sentence about Wordsworth's *Excursion*, and one tasteless sneer at Charles Lamb. Even the mighty figure of Sainte-Beuve totters at the whisper of the name Balzac. Even Matthew Arnold would have been wiser to have taken counsel with himself before he laughed at Shelley. And the very unimportant but sincere and interesting writer, whose book occupies us to-day, is in some respects the crowning instance of the rule. His literary existence has been sacrificed by a single outburst of petulant criticism, which was not even literary, but purely political.

The only passage of Winstanley's *Lives of the English Poets* which is ever quoted is the paragraph which refers to Milton, who, when it appeared, had been dead thirteen years. It runs thus:

"*John Milton* was one whose natural parts might deservedly give him a place amongst the principal of our English Poets, having written two Heroick Poems and a Tragedy, namely *Paradice Lost, Paradice Regain'd*, and *Sampson Agonista*. But his Fame is gone out like a Candle in a Snuff, and his Memory will always stink, which might have ever lived in honourable Repute, had not he been a notorious Traytor, and most impiously and villanously bely'd that blessed Martyr, King *Charles* the First."

Mr. Winstanley does not leave us in any doubt of his own political bias, and his mode is simply infamous. It is the roughest and most unpardonable expression now extant of the prejudice generally felt against Milton in London, after the Restoration--a prejudice which even Dryden, who in his heart knew better, could not wholly resist. This one sentence is all that most readers of seventeenth-century literature know about Winstanley, and it is not surprising that it has created an objection to him. I forget who it was, among the critics of the beginning of this century, who was accustomed to buy copies of the *Lives of the English Poets* wherever he could pick them up, and burn them, in piety to the angry spirit of Milton. This was certainly more sensible conduct than that of the Italian nobleman, who used to build MSS. of Martial into little pyres, and consume them with spices, to express his admiration of Catullus. But no one can wonder that the world has not forgiven Winstanley for that atrocious phrase about Milton's fame having "gone out like a candle in a snuff, so that his memory will always stink." No, Mr. William Winstanley, it is your own name that--smells so very unpleasantly.

Yet I am paradoxical enough to believe that poor Winstanley never wrote these sentences which have destroyed his fame. To support my theory, it is needful to recount the very scanty knowledge we possess of his life. He is said to have been a barber, and to have risen by his exertions with the razor; but, against that legend, is to be posed the fact that on the titles of his earliest books, dedicated to public men who must have known, he styles himself "Gent." The dates of his birth and death are, I believe, a matter of conjecture. But the *Lives of the English Poets* is the latest of his books, and the earliest was published in 1660. This is his *England's Worthies*, a group of what we should call to-day "biographical studies." The longest and the most interesting of these is one on Oliver Cromwell, the tone of which is almost grossly laudatory, although published at the very moment of Restoration. Now, it is a curious, and, at first sight, a very disgraceful fact, that in 1684, when the book of *England's Worthies* was re-issued, all the praise of republicans was cancelled, and abuse substituted for it. And then, in 1687, came the *Lives of the English Poets*, with its horrible attack on Milton. The character of Winstanley seems to be as base as any on literary record. I have come to the conclusion, however, that Winstanley was guilty, neither of retracting what he said about Cromwell, nor of slandering Milton. The black woman excused her husband for not answering the bell, "'Cause he's dead," and the excuse was considered valid. I hope that when these interpolations were made, poor Winstanley was dead.

Any one who reads the *Lives of the English Poets* carefully, will be impressed with two facts: first, that the author had an acquaintance with the early versifiers of Great Britain, which was quite extraordinary, and which can hardly be found at fault by our modern knowledge; while, secondly, that he shows a sudden and unaccountable ignorance of his immediate contemporaries of the younger school. Except Campion, who is a discovery of our own day, not a single Elizabethan or Jacobean rhymester of the second or third rank escapes his notice. Among the writers of a still later generation, I miss no names save those of Vaughan, who was very obscure in his own lifetime, and Marvell, who would be excluded by the same prejudice which mocked at Milton. But among Poets of the Restoration, men and women who were in their full fame in 1687, the omissions are quite startling. Not a word is here about Otway, Lee, or Crowne; Butler is not mentioned, nor the Matchless Orinda, nor Roscommon, nor Sir Charles Sedley. A careful examination of the dates of works which Winstanley refers to, produces a curious result. There is not mentioned, so far as I can trace, a single poem or play which was published later than 1675, although the date on the title-page of the *Lives of the English Poets* is

1687. Rather an elaborate list of Dryden's publications is given, but it stops at *Amboyna* (1673). On this I think it is not too bold to build a theory, which may last until Winstanley's entry of burial is discovered in some country church, that he died soon after 1675. If this were the case, the recantations in his *English Worthies* of 1684 would be so many posthumous outrages committed on his blameless tomb, and the infamous sentence about Milton may well have been foisted into a posthumous volume by the same wicked hand. If we could think that Samuel Manship, at the Sign of the Black Bull, was the obsequious rogue who did it, that would be one more sin to be numbered against the sad race of publishers.

In studying old books about the poets, it sometimes occurs to us to wonder whether the readers of two hundred years ago appreciated the same qualities in good verse which are now admired. Did the ringing and romantic cadences of Shakespeare affect their senses as they do ours? We know that they praised Carew and Suckling, but was it "Ask me no more where June bestows," and "Hast thou seen the down in the air," which gave them pleasure? It would sometimes seem, from the phrases they use and the passages they quote, that if poetry was the same two centuries ago, its readers had very different ears from ours. Of Herrick Winstanley says that he was "one of the Scholars of Apollo of the middle Form, yet something above *George Withers*, in a pretty Flowry and Pastoral Gale of Fancy, in a vernal Prospect of some Hill, Cave, Rock, or Fountain; which but for the interruption of other trivial Passages, might have made up none of the worst Poetick Landskips," and then he quotes, as a sample of Herrick, a tiresome" epigram," in the poet's worst style. This is not delicate or acute criticism, as we judge nowadays; but I would give a good deal to meet Winstanley at a coffee-house, and go through the *Hesperides* with him over a dish of chocolate. It would be wonderfully interesting to discover which passages in Herrick really struck the contemporary mind as "flowery," and which as "trivial." But this is just what all seventeenth-century criticism, even Dryden's, omits to explain to us. The personal note in poetical criticism, the appeal to definite taste, to the experience of eye and ear, is not met with, even in suggestion, until we reach the pamphlets of John Dennis.

The particular copy of Winstanley which lies before me is a valuable one; I owe it to the generosity of a friend in Chicago, who hoards rare books, and yet has the greatness of soul sometimes to part with them. It is interleaved, and the blank pages are rather densely inscribed with notes in the handwriting of Dr. Thomas Percy, the poetical Bishop of Dromore. From his hands it passed into those of John Bowyer Nichols, the antiquary. Percy's notes are little more than references to other authorities, memoranda for one of his own useful compilations, yet it is pleasant to have even a slight personal relic of so admirable a man. Mr. Riviere has bound the volume for me, and I suppose that poor rejected Winstanley exists nowhere else in so elegant a shape.

THE ROMANCE OF A DICTIONARY

HISTOIRE DE L'ACADEMIE FRANCOISE: *avec un Abrege des Vies du Cardinal de Richelieu, Vaugelas, Corneille, Ablancourt, Mezerai, Voiture, Patru, la Fontaine, Boileau, Racine Et autres Illustres Academiciens qui la Composent*. *A La Haye, MDCLXXXVIII*.

It is not often, in these days, when the pastime of bibliography is reduced to a science, that one is rewarded, as one so often was a quarter of a century ago, by picking up an unregarded treasure on the bookstalls. But the other day I really had a pleasant little "find," and it was the reward of virtue. It came of having a tender heart. My eye caught what Mr. Austin Dobson would call "a dear and dumpy twelve," lying open upon other books, face downward, in the most ignominious posture. I saw at a glance, from the tooling on its faded and half-broken back, that it was French and of the seventeenth century, and that somebody had prized it once. I could read the lettering *Academ. Franc*., and I gave the pence which were wanted for it. It proved a most rewarding little volume. It was published at The Hague in 1688, and it was a new edition of the *Histoire de l'Academie Francaise*. A preface says that "for the honour of our nation" (the French, presumably, not the Dutch), the publisher has thought it proper to issue an edition "more correct and more elegant" than has hitherto been seen, brought down to date with many new and curious pieces. Among other things, the said publisher thinks that "the English will not be displeased to see the Panegyric" of King Louis XIV. "admirably rendered in their language by a Person of their Nation." But what immediately caught my attention, and filled me with delight, was an absolutely contemporary account, written specially for this 1688 edition, of the great quarrel between the French Academy and the Abbe Furetiere. Of this I propose to speak to-day.

We live in an age of Dictionaries and Encyclopedias, which we look upon as universal panaceas for culture. There was a similar rage for dictionaries in France two hundred and fifty years ago. We may very rapidly remind ourselves that the French Academy was constituted in 1634 with thirty-five members, who became the stationary and immortal Forty in 1639. One of its original functions was the preparation of a great Dictionary of the French language, under the special care of the eminent grammarian, Vaugelas, who had through his lifetime made collections--"various beautiful and curious observations," as Pellisson calls them--towards a reasoned philological study of French. The poet Chapelain was appointed a sort of general editor of the projected Dictionary, which was solemnly started early in 1638. For the next four years the Academicians were very active, spurred on by Richelieu, but when, in 1642, the Cardinal died, their zeal relented, and when, in 1650, Vaugelas's presence ceased to urge them forward, it flagged altogether. Vaugelas died bankrupt, and his creditors seized his writing-desks, the drawers of which contained a great part of the MS. collections for the Dictionary. It was only after a lawsuit that the Academy recovered those papers, and Mezeray was then set to continue the editing of the work. Still twice a week the Academy met to consult about the Dictionary, but so languidly and with so little fire, that Boisrobert said that not the youngest of the Forty could hope to live to print the letter G. As a matter of fact, not one of those who started the Dictionary lived to see it published.

In this slow fashion, with long Rip Van Winkle slumbers and occasional faint awakenings, the French Academy faltered on with fitful persistence towards the completion of its famous Dictionary. But, as I have said, it was a period of great enthusiasm about all such summaries of knowledge, and Paris was thirsting for grammars, lexicons, inventories of language and the like. The Academy insisted that the world must wait for the approach of their vast and lumbering machine; but meanwhile public curiosity was impatient, and all sorts of brief and imperfect dictionaries were issued to satisfy it. The publication of these spurious guides to knowledge infuriated the Academy, until in 1674 the dog permanently occupied the manger by inducing the King to issue a decree "forbidding all printers and publishers to print any new dictionary of the French language, under any title whatsoever, until the publication of that of the French Academy, or until twenty years have expired since the proclamation of the present decree." This cut the ground from under the feet of all rivals, and the Academy could meet twice a week as before and mumble its definitions with serene assurance. From this false security it was roused by the incident which my "dumpy twelve" recounts.

It was from the very heart of their own body that the great attack upon their privileges unexpectedly fell upon the Academicians. In 1662 they had elected (in the place of De Boissat, a very obscure original member) the Abbe of Chalivoy, Antoine Furetiere. This man, born in Paris of poor parents in 1619, had raised himself to eminence as an Orientalist and grammarian, and was welcomed among the Forty as likely to be particularly helpful to them in their Dictionary work. He was probably one of those men whose true character does not come out until they attain success. But no sooner was Furetiere an Immortal than he began to distinguish himself in unanticipated ways. He proved himself an adept in parody and satire, and so long as he contented himself with laughing at people like Charles Sorel, the author of *Francion*, who had no friends, the Academicians were calm and amused, But Furetiere was not merely the author of that extremely amusing medley, *Le Roman Bourgeois* (1666), which still holds its place in French literature as a minor classic, but he was also a real student of philology, and one of those who most ardently desired to see the settlement of the canon of French language. It incensed him beyond words that his colleagues dawdled so endlessly over their committees and their definitions. He began to make collections of his own, no doubt at first with the perfectly loyal intention of adding them to the common store. Meanwhile he lashed the rest of the Academy with his tongue. Other Academicians did this also, such men as Patru and Boisrobert, but they had not Furetiere's nasty way of putting things. One perceives that about the year 1680 the sarcasms of Furetiere had really become something more than the rest of the Immortals could put up with.

He delivered himself into their hands, and here my little volume takes up the tale. On the 3rd of January, 1685, the French Academy met to mourn the death of its most illustrious member, the great Pierre Corneille, and to elect his younger brother to take his place. While the members were chatting together their Librarian handed about among them copies of a "privilege" which had just been obtained by the Abbe Furetiere to publish "a universal Dictionary containing generally all

French words, old as well as modern, and the terms employed in all arts and sciences." So declares my little book; but it would seem that the officers of the Academy at least a week earlier had their attention drawn to what Furetiere was doing. Perhaps it was not until the election of Thomas Corneille that an opportunity occurred of making the members generally aware of it. One wonders whether Furetiere himself was present on the 3rd of January; if so, what puttings of periwigs together there must have been in corners, and what taps of gold-headed canes on lace-frilled cuffs! It was felt, as my little volume puts it, that "Monsieur the Abbe Furetiere, being one of the Forty Academicians, ought not to have been privately busying himself on a work which he knew to be the principal occupation of the whole Academy." It is surprising, in the face of the monopoly which that body had secured, that Furetiere was able to obtain a Privilege for his own Dictionary, but in all probability, as he was one of the Forty, the censors supposed that he was acting in concert with his colleagues.

Then began a hue and cry with which the learned world of Paris rang for months. Never was such a scandal, never such a rain of pamphlets and lampoons on one side and the other. One has only to glance at the contemporary portraits of Furetiere to see that he was not the man to yield a point; his wrinkled face looks the very mirror of sarcastic obstinacy and brilliant ill-nature. The Academy, in solemn session, appointed Regnier Desmarais, their secretary, to wait on the Chancellor to demand the cancelling of Furetiere's privilege. But the Abbe had powerful friends also, and by their help the Chancellor's action was delayed, while Furetiere hurried out a specimen of his work. He says in the preface that no author ever had a more pressing need for the protection of a prince than he has who sees the labour of years about to be sacrificed to the envy of others. He goes on to explain that he has never dreamed of interfering with the work of the Academy, for which he has the greatest possible respect, but that he only hopes to render service to the public by supplementing its labours. The Academy, in fact, had expressly declined to include in its Dictionary the technical terms of art and science, and it is particularly with these that Furetiere is occupied. His answer to those who accuse him of stealing from the unpublished *cahiers* of the Academy is the uniformity of his work from A to Z; whereas, if he had stolen from his colleagues, he must have stopped at O-P, which was the point they had reached in 1684.

The Academy was not pacified, and began to take counsel how they could turn Furetiere out of their body. There was no precedent for such a degradation, but a parallel was sought for in the fact that the Sorbonne had successfully ejected one of its most famous doctors, Arnauld. Meanwhile the suit went on, the Thirty-nine versus the One. Furetiere is said to have bowed for a moment beneath the storm, offering to blend his work in the general Dictionary of the Academy, or to remove from it all words not admitted to deal technically with art and science. But passion had gone too far, and on the 22nd of January, 1685, at a general meeting, twenty Academicians being present, Furetiere was expelled from the body by a majority of nineteen to one. It is believed that the one who voted for mercy was the most illustrious of all, Racine. Boileau and Bossuet also defended the Abbe, and when the matter became at last so serious that the King himself was obliged to take cognisance of it, it was understood that his sympathies also were with Furetiere.

My little volume (written, I think, in 1687) does not know anything about the expulsion, which was therefore probably secret. It says: "As to Monsieur Furetiere, he no longer puts in an appearance at the meetings of the Academy, but it is not known whether any other Academician is to be elected in his place." As a matter of fact, the society hesitated to go so far as this, and the seat was left vacant. Not for long, however; the unanimous rancour of so many men of influence and rank had successfully ruined the fortune and broken the spirit of the old piratical lexicographer. Before retiring into private life, however, he poured out in his ***Couches de l'Academie*** a torrent of poison, which was distilled through the presses of Amsterdam in 1687. One of his earlier colleagues at the Academy supplied the bankrupt man with the necessaries of life, until, on the 14th of May, 1688, probably just as the "dumpy twelve" was passing through the press, he died in Paris like a rat in a hole. His Dictionary, being suppressed in France, was edited, after his death, in 1690, at The Hague and Rotterdam, and enjoyed a great success. We learn from a letter of Racine to Boileau that in 1694 the publisher ventured to offer a copy of a new edition of it to the King of France, and that it was graciously received. If the poor old man could have struggled on a little longer he might have lived to see himself become fashionable and successful again.

With all his misfortunes he managed to beat the Academy, for that body, in spite of its superhuman efforts, did not contrive to publish its Dictionary till four years after the appearance of Furetiere's. The latter is a great curiosity of lexicography, a vast storehouse of peculiar and rare information. It is always consulted by scholars, but never without a recollection of the extraordinary struggle which its author sustained, singlehanded, against the world, and in which he fell, overpowered by numbers, only to triumph after all in the ashes of his fame.

LADY WINCHILSEA'S POEMS

MISCELLANY POEMS. With Two Plays. By Ardelia.
  I never list presume to Parnass hill, But piping low, in shade of lowly grove, I play to please myself, albeit ill.
Spencer Shep. Cal. June.
Manuscript in folio. Circa 1696.

There is no other book in my library to which I feel that I possess so clear a presumptive right as to this manuscript. Other rare volumes would more fitly adorn the collections of bibliophiles more learned, more ingenious, more elegant, than I. But if there is any person in the two hemispheres who has so fair a claim upon the ghost of Ardelia, let that man stand forth. Ardelia was uncultivated and unsung when I constituted myself, years ago, her champion. With the exception of a noble fragment of laudation from Wordsworth, no discriminating praise from any modern critic had stirred the ashes of her name. I made it my business to insist in many places on the talent of Ardelia. I gave her, for the first time, a chance of challenging public taste, by presenting to readers of Mr. Ward's **English Poets** many pages of extracts from her writings; and I hope it is not indiscreet to say that, when the third volume of that compilation appeared, Mr. Matthew Arnold told me that its greatest revelation to himself had been the singular merit of this lady. Such being my claim on the consideration of Ardelia, no one will, I think, grudge me the possession of this unknown volume of her works in manuscript. It came into my hands by a strange coincidence. In his brief life of Anne Finch, Countess of Winchilsea-- for that was Ardelia's real name--Theophilus Gibber says, "A great number of our authoress' poems still continue unpublished, in the hands of the Rev. Mr. Creake." In 1884 I saw advertised, in an obscure book-list, a folio volume of old manuscript poetry. Something excited my curiosity, and I sent for it. It proved to be a vast collection of the poems of my beloved Anne Finch. I immediately communicated with the bookseller, and asked him whence it came. He replied that it had been sold, with furniture, pictures and books, at the dispersing of the effects of a family of the name of Creake. Thank you, divine Ardelia! It was well done; it was worthy of you.

Anne Finch, Countess of Winchilsea, is not a commanding figure in history, but she is an isolated and a well-defined one. She is what one of the precursors of Shakespeare calls "a diminutive excelsitude." She was entirely out of sympathy with her age, and her talent was hampered and suppressed by her conditions. She was the solitary writer of actively developed romantic tastes between Marvell and Gray, and she was not strong enough to create an atmosphere for herself within the vacuum in which she languished. The facts of her life are extremely scanty, although they may now be considerably augmented by the help of my folio. She was born about 1660, the daughter of a Hampshire baronet. She was maid of honour to Mary of Modena, Duchess of York, and at Court she met Heneage Finch, who was gentleman of the bed-chamber to the Duke. They married in 1685, probably on the occasion of the enthronement of their master and mistress, and when the crash came in 1688, they fled together to the retirement of Eastwell Park. They inhabited this mansion for the rest of their lives, although it was not until the death of his nephew, in 1712, that Heneage Finch became fourth Earl of Winchilsea. In 1713 Anne was at last persuaded to publish a selection of her poems, and in 1720 she died. The Earl survived her until 1726.

My manuscript was written, I think, in or about the year 1696--that is to say, when Mrs. Finch was in retirement from the Court. She has adopted the habit of writing,

Betrayed by solitude to try

Amusements, which the prosperous fly.

But her exile from the world gives her no disquietude. It seems almost an answer to her prayer. Years before, when she was at the centre of fashion in the Court of James II., she had written in an epistle to the Countess of Thanet:

Give me, O indulgent Fate,

Give me yet, before I die,

A sweet, but absolute retreat,

'Mongst paths so lost, and trees so high,
That the world may ne'er invade,
Through such windings and such shade,
My unshaken liberty.

This was a sentiment rarely expressed and still more rarely felt by English ladies at the close of the seventeenth century. What their real opinion usually was is
clothed in crude and ready language by the heroines of Wycherley and Shadwell.
Like Lucia, in the comedy of **Epsom Wells**, to live out of London was to live in a
wilderness, with bears and wolves as one's companions. Alone in that age Anne
Finch truly loved the country, for its own sake, and had an eye to observe its features.

She had one trouble, constitutional low spirits: she was a terrible sufferer from
what was then known as "The Spleen." She wrote a long pindaric Ode on the Spleen,
which was printed in a miscellany in 1701, and was her first introduction to the
public. She talks much about her melancholy in her verses, but, with singular good
sense, she recognised that it was physical, and she tried various nostrums. Neither
tea, nor coffee, nor ratafia did her the least service:

In vain to chase thee every art I try,
In vain all remedies apply,
In vain the Indian leaf infuse,
Or the parched eastern berry bruise,
Or pass, in vain, those bounds, and nobler liquors use.

Her neurasthenia threw a cloud over her waking hours, and took sleep from
her eyelids at night:

How shall I woo thee, gentle Rest,
To a sad mind, with cares oppress'd?
By what soft means shall I invite
Thy powers into my soul to-night?
Yet, gentle Sleep, if thou wilt come,
Such darkness shall prepare the room
As thy own palace overspreads,--
Thy palace stored with peaceful beds,--
And Silence, too, shall on thee wait

Deep, as in the Turkish State;
Whilst, still as death, I will be found,
My arms by one another bound,
And my dull limbs so clos'd shall be
As if already seal'd by thee.

She tried a course of the waters at Tunbridge Wells, but without avail. When the abhorred fit came on, the world was darkened to her. Only two things could relieve her--the soothing influence of solitude with nature and the Muses, or the sympathetic presence of her husband. She disdained the little feminine arts of her age:

Nor will in fading silks compose
Faintly the inimitable rose,
Fill up an ill-drawn bird, or paint on glass
The Sovereign's blurr'd and indistinguished face,
The threatening angel and the speaking ass.

But she will wander at sundown through the exquisite woods of Eastwell, and will watch the owlets in their downy nest or the nightingale silhouetted against the fading sky. Then her constitutional depression passes, and she is able once more to be happy:

Our sighs are then but vernal air,
But April-drops our tears,

as she says in delicious numbers that might be Wordsworth's own. In these delightful moments, released from the burden of her tyrant malady, her eyes seem to have been touched with the herb euphrasy, and she has the gift, denied to the rest of her generation, of seeing nature and describing what she sees. In these moods, this contemporary of Dryden and Congreve gives us such accurate transcripts of country life as the following:

When the loos'd horse now, as his pasture leads,
Comes slowly grazing through the adjoining meads,
Whose stealing face and lengthened shade we fear,
Till torn-up forage in his teeth we hear;
When nibbling sheep at large pursue their food,
And unmolested kine rechew the cud:

When curlews cry beneath the village-walls,
And to her straggling brood the partridge calls.

In Eastwell Park there was a hill, called Parnassus, to which she was particularly partial, and to this she commonly turned her footsteps.

Melancholy as she was, however, and devoted to reverie, she could be gay enough upon occasion, and her sprightly poems have a genuine sparkle. Here is an anacreontic--written "for my brother Leslie Finch"--which has never before been printed:

From the Park, and the Play,
And Whitehall, come away
To the Punch-bowl by far more inviting;
To the fops and 'the beaux
Leave those dull empty shows,
And see here what is truly delighting.
   The half globe 'tis in figure,
And would it were bigger,
Yet here's the whole universe floating;
Here's titles and places,
Rich lands, and fair faces,
And all that is worthy our doting.
   'Twas a world like to this
The hot Grecian did miss,
Of whom histories keep such a pother;
To the bottom he sunk,
And when he had drunk,
Grew maudlin, and wept for another.

At another point, Anne Finch bore very little likeness to her noisy sisterhood of fashion. In an age when it was the height of ill-breeding for a wife to admit a partiality for her husband, Ardelia was not ashamed to confess that Daphnis--for so she styled the excellent Heneage Finch--absorbed every corner of her mind that was not occupied by the Muses. It is a real pleasure to transcribe, for the first time since they were written on the 2nd of April, 1685, these honest couplets:

This, to the crown and blessing of my life,

The much-loved husband of a happy wife;
To him whose constant passion found the art
To win a stubborn and ungrateful heart;
And to the world by tenderest proof discovers
They err who say that husbands can't be lovers.
With such return of passion as is due,
Daphnis I love, Daphnis my thoughts pursue,
Daphnis, my hopes, my joys are bounded all in you!

Nearly thirty years later the same accent is audible, thinned a little by advancing years, and subdued from passion to tenderness, yet as genuine as at first. When at length the Earl began to suffer from the gout, his faithful family songster recorded that also in her amiable verse, and prayed that "the bad disease"

May you but brief unfrequent visits find
To prove you patient, your Ardelia kind.

No one can read her sensitive verses, and not be sure that she was the sweetest and most soothing of bed-side visitants.

It was a quiet life which Daphnis and Ardelia spent in the recesses of Eastwell Park. They saw little company and paid few visits. There was a stately excursion now and then, to the hospitable Thynnes at Longleat, and Anne Finch seldom omitted to leave behind her a metrical tribute to the beauties of that mansion. They seem to have kept up little connection with the Court or with London. There is no trace of literary society in this volume. Nicholas Rowe twice sent down for their perusal translations which he had made; and from another source we learn that Lady Winchilsea had a brisk passage of compliments with Pope. But these were rare incidents. We have rather to think of the long years spent in the seclusion of Eastwell, by these gentle impoverished people of quality, the husband occupied with his mathematical studies, his painting, the care of his garden; the wife studying further afield in her romantic reverie, watching the birds in wild corners of her park, carrying her Tasso, hidden in a fold of her dress, to a dell so remote that she forgets the way back, and has to be carried home "in a Water-cart driven by one of the Underkeepers in his green Coat, with a Hazle-bough for a Whip." It is a little oasis of delicate and pensive refinement in that hot close of the seventeenth century, when so many unseemly monsters were bellowing in the social wilderness.

AMASIA

AMASIA: *or, The Works of the Muses. A Collection of Poems. In three volumes. By Mr. John Hopkins. London: Printed by Tho. Warren, for Bennet Banbury, at the Blue-Anchor, in the Lower-Walk of the New-Exchange*, 1700.

It has often been remarked that if the author of the poorest collection of minor verse would accurately relate in his quavering numbers what his personal observations and adventures have been, his book would not be entirely without value. But ninety-nine times out of a hundred, this is precisely what he cannot do. His rhymes carry him whither he would not, and he is lost in a fog of imitated phrases and spurious sensations. The very odd and very rare set of three little volumes, which now come before us, offer a curious exception to this rule. The author of *Amasia* was no poet, but he possessed the faculty of writing with exactitude about himself. He prattled on in heroic couplets from hour to hour, recording the tiny incidents of his life. At first sight, his voluble miscellany seems a mere wilderness of tame verses, but when we examine it closely a story gradually evolves. We come to know John Hopkins, and live in the intimacy of his circle. His poems contain a novelette in solution. So far as I can discover, nothing whatever is known of him save what he reveals of himself, and no one, I think, has ever searched his three uninviting volumes. In the following paragraphs I have put together his story as it is to be found in the pages of *Amasia*.

By a single allusion to the *Epistolary Poems* of Charles Hopkins, "very well perform'd by my Brother," in 1694, we are able to identify the author of *Amasia* with certainty. He was the second son of the Right Rev. Ezekiel Hopkins, Lord Bishop of Derry. The elder brother whom we have mentioned, Charles, was considerably his senior; for six years the latter occupied a tolerably prominent place in London literary society, was the intimate friend of Dryden and Congreve, published three or four plays not without success, and possessed a name which is pretty frequently met with in books of the time. But to John Hopkins I have discovered scarcely an allusion. He does not seem to have moved in his brother's circle, and his society was probably more courtly than literary. If we may trust his own account the author of *Amasia* was born, doubtless at Londonderry, on the 1st of January, 1675. He was, therefore, only twenty-five when his poems were published, and the exquisitely affected portrait which adorns the first volume must represent him as younger still, since it was executed by the Dutch engraver, F.H. van Hove, who was found murdered in October, 1698.

Pause a moment, dear reader, and observe Mr. John Hopkins, *alias* Sylvius, set out with all the artillery of ornament to storm the heart of Amasia. Notice his embroidered silken coat, his splendid lace cravat, the languishment of his large foolish eyes, the indubitable touch of Spanish red on those smooth cheeks. But, above all contemplate the wonders of his vast peruke. He has a name, be sure, for every portion of that killing structure. Those sausage-shaped curls, close to the ears, are *confidants*; those that dangle round the temples, *favorites*; the sparkling lock that descends alone over the right eyebrow is the *passagere*; and, above all, the gorgeous knot that unites the curls and descends on the left breast, is aptly named the *meurtriere*. If he would but turn his head, we should see his *creves-coeur*, the two delicate curled locks at the nape of his neck. The escutcheon below his portrait bears, very suitably, three loaded muskets rampant. Such was Sylvius, conquering but, alas! not to conquer.

The youth of John Hopkins was passed in the best Irish society. His father, the Bishop, married--apparently in second nuptials, for John speaks not of her as a man speaks of his mother--the daughter of the Earl of Radnor. Lady Araminta Hopkins seems to have been a friend of Isabella, Duchess of Grafton, the exquisite girl who, at the age of five, had married a bridegroom of nine, and at twenty-three was left a widow, to be the first toast in English society. The poems of John Hopkins are dedicated to this Dowager-duchess, who, when they were published, had already for two years been the wife of Sir Thomas Hanmer. At the age of twelve, and probably in Dublin, Hopkins met the mysterious lady who animates these volumes under the name of Amasia. Who was Amasia? That, alas! even the volubility of her lover does not reveal. But she was Irish, the daughter of a wealthy and perhaps titled personage, and the intimate companion for many years of the beautiful Duchess of Grafton.

Love did not begin at first sight. Sylvius played with Amasia when they both were children, and neither thought of love. Later on, in early youth, the poet was devoted only to a male friend, one Martin. To him ecstatic verses are inscribed:

O Martin! Martin! let the grateful sound

Reach to that Heav'n which has our Friendship crown'd,

And, like our endless Friendship, meet no bound.

But alas! one day Martin came back, after a long absence, and, although he still

With generous, kind, continu'd Friendship burn'd,

he found Sylvius entirely absorbed by Amasia. Martin knew better than to show temper; he accepted the situation, and

the lov'd Amasia's Health flew round,

Amasia's Health the Golden Goblets crown'd.

Now began the first and happiest portion of the story. Amasia had no suspicion of the feelings of the poet, and he was only too happy to be permitted to watch her movements. He records, in successive copies of verses, the various things she did. He seems to have been on terms of delightful intimacy with the lady, and he calls all sorts of people of the highest position to witness how he suffered. To Lady Sandwich are dedicated poems on "Amasia, drawing her own Picture," on "Amasia, playing with a Clouded Fan," on "Amasia, singing, and sticking pins in a Red Silk Pincushion." We are told how Amasia "looked at me through a Multiplying-Glass," how she was troubled with a redness in her eyes, how she danced before a looking-glass, how her flowered muslin nightgown (or "night-rail," as he calls it) took fire, and how, though she promised to sing, yet she never performed. We have a poem on the circumstance that Amasia, "having prick'd me with a Pin, accidentally scratched herself with it;" and another on her "asking me if I slept well after so tempestuous a night." But perhaps the most intimate of all is a poem "To Amasia, tickling a Gentleman." It was no perfunctory tickling that Amasia administered:

While round his sides your nimble Fingers played, With pleasing softness did they swiftly rove, While, at each touch, they made his Heart-strings move. As round his Breast, his ravish'd Breast they crowd, We hear their Musick when he laughs aloud.

This is probably the only instance in literature in which a gentleman has complacently celebrated in verse the fact that his lady-love has tickled some other gentleman.

But this generous simplicity was not long to last. In 1690 Hopkins's father, the Bishop, had died. We may conjecture that Lady Araminta took charge of the boy, and that his home, in vacation time, was with her in Dublin or London. He writes like a youth who has always been petted; the *frou-frou* of fine ladies' petticoats is heard in all his verses. But he had no fortune and no prospects; he was utterly, he confesses, without ambition. The stern papa of Amasia had no notion of bestowing her on the penniless Sylvius, and when the latter began to court her in earnest, she rebuffed him. She tore up his love-letters, she teased him by sending her black page to the window when he was ogling for her in the street below, she told him he was too young for her, and although she had no objection to his addressing verses to her, she gave him no serious encouragement. She was to be married, he hints, to some one of her own rank--some rich "country booby."

At last, early in 1698, in company with the Duchess of Grafton, and possibly on the occasion of the second marriage of the latter, Amasia was taken off to France, and Hopkins never saw her again. A year later he received news of her death, and his little romance was over. He became ill, and Dr. Gibbons, the great fashionable physician of the day, was called in to attend him. The third volume closes by his summoning the faithful and unupbraiding Martin back to his heart:

Love lives in Sun-Shine, or that Storm, Despair,
But gentler Friendship Breathes a Mod'rate Air.

And so Sylvius, with all his galaxy of lovely Irish ladies, his fashionable Muses, and his trite and tortured fancy, disappears into thin air.

The only literary man whom he mentions as a friend is George Farquhar, himself a native of Londonderry, and about the same age as Hopkins. This playwright seems to be sometimes alluded to as Daphnis, sometimes under his own name. Before the performance of *Love and a Bottle*, Hopkins prophesied for the author a place where

Congreve, Vanbrook, and Wicherley must sit,
The great Triumvirate of Comick Wit,

and later on he thought that even Collier himself ought to commend the *Constant Couple, or A Trip to the Jubilee*. At the first performance of this play, towards the close of 1699, Hopkins was greatly perturbed by the presence of a lady who reminded him of Amasia, and when he visited the theatre next he was less pleased with the play. He had a vague and infelicitous scheme for turning **Paradise Lost** into rhyme. These are the only traces of literary bias. In other respects Hopkins is interested in nothing more serious than a lock of Amasia's hair; the china cup she had, "round the sides of which were painted Trees, and at the bottom a Naked Woman Weeping;" her box of patches, in which she finds a silver penny; or the needlework embroidered on her gown. When Amasia died there was no reason why Sylvius should continue to exist, and he fades out of our vision like a ghost.

LOVE AND BUSINESS

LOVE AND BUSINESS: *in a Collection of occasionary Verse and epistolary Prose not hitherto published. By Mr. George Farquhar*. En Orenge il n'y a point d'oranges. **London, printed for B. Lintott, at the Post-House, in the Middle Temple-Gate, Fleet Street**. 1702.

There are some books, like some people, of whom we form an indulgent opinion without finding it easy to justify our liking. The young man who went to the life-insurance office and reported that his father had died of no particular disease, but just of "plain death," would sympathise with the feeling I mention. Sometimes we like a book, not for any special merit, but just because it is what it is. The rare, and yet not celebrated, miscellany of which I am about to write has this character. It is not instructive, or very high-toned, or exceptionally clever, but if it were a man, all people that are not prigs would say that it was a very good sort of fellow. If it be, as it certainly is, a literary advantage for a nondescript collection of trifles, to reproduce minutely the personality of its writer, then **Love and Business** has one definite merit. Wherever we dip into its pages we may use it as a telephone, and hear a young Englishman, of the year 1700, talking to himself and to his friends in the most unaffected accents.

Captain George Farquhar, in 1702, was four-and-twenty years of age. He was a smart, soldier-like Irishman, of "a splenetic and amorous complexion," half an actor, a quarter a poet, and altogether a very honest and gallant gentleman. He had taken to the stage kindly enough, and at twenty-one had written **Love and a**

Bottle. Since then, two other plays, **The Constant Couple** and **Sir Harry Wildair**, had proved that he had wit and fancy, and knew how to knit them together into a rattling comedy. But he was poor, always in pursuit of that timid wild-fowl, the occasional guinea, and with no sort of disposition to settle down into a heavy citizen. In order to bring down a few brace of golden game, he shovels into Lintott's hands his stray verses of all kinds, a bundle of letters he wrote from Holland, a dignified essay or discourse upon Comedy, and, with questionable taste perhaps, a set of copies of the love-letters he had addressed to the lady who became his wife. All this is not very praiseworthy, and as a contribution to literature it is slight indeed; but, then, how genuine and sincere, how guileless and picturesque is the self-revelation of it! There is no attempt to make things better than they are, nor any pandering to a cynical taste by making them worse. Why should he conceal or falsify? The town knows what sort of a fellow George Farquhar is. Here are some letters and some verses; the beaux at White's may read them if they will, and then throw them away.

As we turn the desultory pages, the figure of the author rises before us, good-natured, easygoing, high-coloured, not bad-looking, with an air of a gentleman in spite of his misfortunes. We do not know the exact details of his military honours. We may think of him as swaggering in scarlet regimentals, but we have his own word for it that he was often in *mufti*. His mind is generally dressed, he says, like his body, in black; for though he is so brisk a spark in company, he suffers sadly from the spleen when he is alone. We can follow him pretty closely through his day. He is a queer mixture of profanity and piety, of coarseness and loyalty, of cleverness and density; we do not breed this kind of beau nowadays, and yet we might do worse, for this specimen is, with all his faults, a man. He dresses carefully in the morning, in his uniform or else in his black suit. When he wants to be specially smart, as, for instance, when he designs a conquest at a birthday-party, he has to ferret among the pawnbrokers for scraps of finery, or secure on loan a fair, full-bottom wig. But he is not so impoverished that he cannot on these occasions give his valet and his barber plenty of work to do preparing his face with razors, perfumes and washes. He would like to be Sir Fopling Flutter, if he could afford it, and gazes a little enviously at that noble creature in his French clothes, as he lounges luxuriantly past him in his coach with six before and six behind.

Poor Captain Farquhar begins to expect that he himself will never be "a first-rate Beau." So, on common mornings, a little splenetic, he wanders down to the coffee-houses and reads the pamphlets, those which find King William glorious, and those that rail at the watery Dutch. He will even be a little Jacobitish for pure foppery, and have a fling at the Church, but in his heart he is with the Ministry. He meets a friend at White's, and they adjourn presently to the Fleece Tavern, where the drawer brings them a bottle of New French and a neat's tongue, over which they discuss the doctrine of predestination so hotly that two mackerel-vendors burst in, mistaking their lifted voices for a cry for fish. His friend has business in the city, and so our poet strolls off to the Park, and takes a turn in the Mall with his hat in his hand, prepared for an adventure or a chat with a friend. Then comes the play, the inevitable early play, still, even in 1700, apt to be so rank-lipped that respectable ladies could only appear at it in masks. It was the transition period, and poor Comedy, who was saying good-bye to literature, was just about to console herself with modesty.

However, a domino may slip aside, and Mr. George Farquhar notices a little lady in a deep mourning mantua, whose eyes are not to be forgotten. She goes, however; it is useless to pursue her; but the music raises his soul to such a pitch of passion that he is almost melancholy. He strolls out into Spring Garden, but there, "with envious eyes, I saw every Man pick up his Mate, whilst I alone walked like solitary Adam before the Creation of his Eve; but the place was no Paradise to me; nothing I found entertaining but the Nightingale." So that in those sweet summer evenings of 1700, over the laced and brocaded couples promenading in Spring Garden, as over good Sir Roger twelve years later, the indulgent nightingale still poured her notes. To-day you cannot hear the very bells of St. Martin's for the roar of the traffic. So lonely, and too easily enamoured, George has to betake himself to the tavern, and a passable Burgundy. There is no idealism about him. He is very fit for repentance next morning. "The searching Wine has sprung the Rheumatism in my Right Hand, my Head aches, my Stomach pukes." Our poor, good-humoured beau has no constitution for this mode of life, and we know, though happily he dreams not of it, that he is to die before he reaches thirty.

This picture of Farquhar's life is nowhere given in the form just related, but not one touch in the portrait but is to be found somewhere in the frank and easy pages of **Love and Business**. The poems are of their age and kind. There is a "Pindarick," of course; it was so easy to write one, and so reputable. There are compliments in verse to one of the female wits who were writing then for the stage, Mrs. Trotter, author of the **Fatal Friendship**; there are amatory explanations of all kinds. When he fails to keep an appointment with a lady on account of the rain--for there were no umbrellas in those days--he likens himself to Leander, wistful on the Sestian shore. He is not always very discreet; Damon's thoughts when "Night's black Curtain o'er the World was spread" were very innocent, but such as we have decided nowadays to say nothing about. It was the fashion of the time to be outspoken. There is no value, however, in the verse, except that it is graphic now and then. The letters are much more interesting. Those sent from Holland in the autumn of 1700 are very good reading. I make bold to quote one passage from the first, describing the storm he encountered in crossing. It depicts our hero to the life, with all his inconsistencies. He says: "By a kind of Poetical Philosophy I bore up pretty well under my Apprehensions; though never worse prepared for Death, I must confess, for I think I never had so much Money about me at a time. We had some Ladies aboard, that were so extremely sick, that they often wished for Death, but were damnably afraid of being drown'd. But, as the Scripture says, 'Sorrow may last for a Night, but Joy cometh in the Morning,'" and so on. The poor fellow means no harm by all this, as Hodgson once said of certain remarks of Byron's.

The love-letters are very curious. It is believed that the sequel of them was a very unhappy marriage. Captain Farquhar was of a loving disposition, and as inflammable as a hay-rick. He cannot have been much more than twenty-one when he described what he desired in a wife. "O could I find," he said--

> O could I find (Grant, Heaven, that once I may!)
> A Nymph fair, kind, poetical and gay
> Whose Love should blaze, unsullied and divine.
> Lighted at first by the bright Lamp of mine.
> Free as a Mistress, faithful as a wife.
> And one that lov'd a Fiddle as her Life,
> Free from all sordid Ends, from Interest free,
> For my own Sake affecting only me,

What a blest Union should our Souls combine!
I hers alone, and she be only mine!

It does not seem a very exacting ideal, but the poor poet missed it. Whether Mrs. Farquhar loved a fiddle as her life is not recorded, but she certainly was not free from all sordid ends and unworthy tricks. The little lady in the mourning mantua soon fell in love with our gallant spark, and when he made court to her, she represented herself as very wealthy. The deed accomplished, Mrs. Farquhar turned out to be penniless; and the poet, like a gentleman as he was, never reproached her, but sat down cheerfully to a double poverty. In *Love and Business* the story does not proceed so far. He receives Miss Penelope V----'s timid advances, describes himself to her, is soon as much in love with his little lady as she with him, and is making broad demands and rich-blooded confidences in fine style, no offence taken where no harm is meant. In one of the letters to Penelope we get a very interesting glance at a famous, and, as it happens, rather obscure, event--the funeral of the great Dryden, in May 1700. Farquhar says:

"I come now from Mr. Dryden's Funeral, where we had an Ode in Horace sung, instead of David's Psalms; whence you may find that we don't think a Poet worth Christian Burial; the Pomp of the Ceremony was a kind of Rhapsody, and fitter, I think, for Hudibras than him; because the Cavalcade was mostly Burlesque; but he was an extraordinary Man, and bury'd after an extraordinary Fashion; for I believe there was never such another Burial seen; the Oration indeed was great and ingenious, worthy the Subject, and like the Author [Dr. Garth], whose Prescriptions can restore the Living, and his Pen embalm the Dead. And so much for Mr. Dryden, whose Burial was the same with his Life,--Variety, and not of a Piece. The Quality and Mob, Farce and Heroicks, the Sublime and Ridicule mixt in a Piece, great Cleopatra in a Hackney Coach."

WHAT ANN LANG READ

Who was Ann Lang? Alas! I am not sure; but she flourished one hundred and sixty years ago, under his glorious Majesty, George I., and I have become the happy possessor of a portion of her library. It consists of a number of cheap novels, all published in 1723 and 1724, when Ann Lang probably bought them; and each carries, written on the back of the title, "ann Lang book 1727," which is doubtless the date of her lending them to some younger female friend. The letters of this inscription are round and laboriously shaped, while the form is always the same, and never "Ann Lang, her book," which is what one would expect. It is not the hand of a person of quality: I venture to conclude that she who wrote it was a milliner's apprentice or a servant-girl. There are five novels in this little collection, and a play, and a pamphlet of poems, and a bundle of love-letters, all signed upon their title-pages by the Ouida of the period, the great Eliza Haywood.

No one who has not dabbled among old books knows how rare have become the strictly popular publications of a non-literary kind which a generation of the lower middle class has read and thrown away. Eliza Haywood lives in the minds of men solely through one very coarse and cruel allusion to her made by Pope in the ***Dunciad***. She was never recognised among people of intellectual quality; she ardently desired to belong to literature, but her wish was never seriously gratified, even by her friend Aaron Hill. Yet she probably numbered more readers, for a year or two, than any other person in the British realm. She poured forth what she called "little Performances" from a tolerably respectable press; and the wonder is that in these days her abundant writings are so seldom to be met with. The secret doubtless is that her large public consisted almost wholly of people like Ann Lang. Eliza was read by servants in the kitchen, by seamstresses, by basket-women, by 'prentices of all sorts, male and female, but mostly the latter. For girls of this sort there was no other reading of a light kind in 1724. It was Eliza Haywood or nothing. The men of the same class read Defoe; but he, with his cynical severity, his absence of all pity for a melting mood, his savagery towards women, was not likely to be preferred by "straggling nymphs." The footman might read ***Roxana***, and the hackney-writer sit up after his toil over ***Moll Flanders***; there was much in these romances to interest men. But what had Ann Lang to do with stories so cold and harsh? She read Eliza Haywood.

But most of her sisters, of Eliza's great *clientele*, did not know how to treat a book. They read it to tatters, and they threw it away. It may be news to some readers that these early novels were very cheap. Ann Lang bought ***Love in Excess***, which is quite a thick volume, for two shillings; and the first volume of **Idalia** (for Eliza was Ouidaesque even in her titles) only cost her eighteen-pence. She seems to have been a clean girl. She did not drop warm lard on the leaves. She did not tottle up her milk-scores on the bastard-title. She did not scribble in the margin "Emanuella is a foul wench." She did not dog's-ear her little library, or stain it, or tear it. I owe it to that rare and fortunate circumstance of her neatness that her beloved books have come into my possession after the passage of so many generations. It must be recollected that Eliza Haywood lived in the very twilight of English fiction. Sixteen years were still to pass, in 1724, before the British novel properly began to dawn in **Pamela**, twenty-five years before it broke in the full splendour of **Tom Jones**. Eliza Haywood simply followed where, two generations earlier, the redoubtable Mrs. Aphra Behn had led. She preserved the old romantic manner, a kind of corruption of the splendid Scudery and Calprenede folly of the middle of the seventeenth century. All that distinguished her was her vehement exuberance and the emptiness of the field. Ann Lang was young, and instinctively attracted to the study of the passion of love. She must read something, and there was nothing but Eliza Haywood for her to read.

The heroines of these old stories were all palpitating with sensibility, although that name had not yet been invented to describe their condition. When they received a letter beginning "To the divine Lassellia," or "To the incomparable Donna Emanuella," they were thrown into the most violent disorder; "a thousand different Passions succeeded one another in their turns," and as a rule "'twas all too sudden to admit disguise." When a lady in Eliza Haywood's novels receives a note from a gentleman, "all her Limbs forget their Function, and she sinks fainting on the Bank, in much the same posture as she was before she rais'd herself a little to take the Letter." I am positive that Ann Lang practised this series of attitudes in the solitude of her garret.

There is no respite for the emotions from Eliza's first page to her last. The implacable Douxmoure (for such was her singular name) "continued for some time in a Condition little different from Madness; but when Reason had a little recovered its usual Sway, a deadly Melancholy succeeded Passion." When Bevillia tried to explain to her cousin that Emilius was no fit suitor for her hand, the young lady swooned twice before she seized Bevillia's "cruel meaning;" and then--ah! then--

"silent the stormy Passions roll'd in her tortured Bosom, disdaining the mean Ease of raging or complaining. It was a considerable time before she utter'd the least Syllable; and when she did, she seem'd to start as from some dreadful Dream, and cry'd, 'It is enough--in knowing one I know the whole deceiving Sex'"; and she began to address an imaginary Women's Rights Meeting.

Plot was not a matter about which Eliza Haywood greatly troubled herself. A contemporary admirer remarked, with justice:

'Tis Love Eliza's soft Affections fires; Eliza writes, but Love alone inspires; 'Tis Love that gives D'Elmont his manly Charms, And tears Amena from her Father's Arms.

These last-named persons are the hero and heroine of ***Love in Excess; or The Fatal Inquiry***, which seems to have been the most popular of the whole series. This novel might be called ***Love Through a Window***; for it almost entirely consists of a relation of how the gentleman prowled by moonlight in a garden, while the lady, in an agitated disorder, peeped out of her lattice in "a most charming Dishabillee." Alas! there was a lock to the door of a garden staircase, and while the lady "was paying a Compliment to the Recluse, he was dextrous enough to slip the Key out of the Door unperceived." Ann Lang!--"a sudden cry of Murder, and the noise of clashing Swords," come none too soon to save those blushes which, we hope, you had in readiness for the turning of the page! Eliza Haywood assures us, in ***Idalia***, that her object in writing is that "the Warmth and Vigour of Youth may be temper'd by a due Consideration"; yet the moralist must complain that she goes a strange way about it. Idalia herself was "a lovely Inconsiderate" of Venice, who escaped in a "Gondula" up "the River Brent," and set all Vicenza by the ears through her "stock of Haughtiness, which nothing could surmount." At last, after adventures which can scarcely have edified Ann Lang, Idalia abruptly "remember'd to have heard of a Monastery at Verona," and left Vicenza at break of day, taking her "unguarded languishments" out of that city and out of the novel. It is true that Ann Lang, for 2s., bought a continuation of the career of Idalia; but we need not follow her.

The perusal of so many throbbing and melting romances must necessarily have awakened in the breast of female readers a desire to see the creator of these tender scenes. I am happy to inform my readers that there is every reason to believe that Ann Lang gratified this innocent wish. At all events, there exists among her volumes the little book of the play sold at the doors of Drury Lane Theatre, when, in the summer of 1724, Eliza Haywood's new comedy of *A Wife to be Lett* was acted there, with the author performing in the part of Mrs. Graspall. The play itself is wretched, and tradition says that it owed what little success it enjoyed to the eager desire which the novelist's readers felt to gaze upon her features. She was about thirty years of age at the time; but no one says that she was handsome, and she was undoubtedly a bad actress, I think the disappointment that evening at the Theatre Royal opened the eyes of Ann Lang. Perhaps it was the appearance of Eliza in the flesh which prevented her old admirer from buying *The Secret History of Cleomina, suppos'd dead*, which I miss from the collection.

If Ann Lang lived on until the publication of *Pamela*--especially if during the interval she had bettered her social condition--with what ardour must she have hailed the advent of what, with all its shortcomings, was a book worth gold. Perhaps she went to Vauxhall with it in her muff, and shook it triumphantly at some middle-aged lady of her acquaintance. Perhaps she lived long enough to see one great novel after another break forth to lighten the darkness of life. She must have looked back on the pompous and lascivious pages of Eliza Haywood, with their long-drawn palpitating intrigues, with positive disgust. The English novel began in 1740, and after that date there was always something wholesome for Ann Lang and her sisters to read.

CATS

LES CHATS. *A Rotterdam, chez Jean Daniel Beman, MDCCXXVIII.*
An accomplished lady of my acquaintance tells me that she is preparing an anthology of the cat. This announcement has reminded me of one of the oddest and most entertaining volumes in my library. People who collect prints of the eighteenth century know an engraving which represents a tom-cat, rampant, holding up an oval portrait of a gentleman and standing, in order to do so, on a volume. The volume is *Les Chats*, the book before us, and the portrait is that of the author, the amiable and amusing Augustin Paradis de Moncrif. He was the son of English, or more probably of Scotch parents settled in Paris, where he was born in 1687. All we

know of his earlier years is to be found in a single sparkling page of d'Alembert, who makes Moncrif float out of obscurity like the most elegant of iridescent bubbles. He was handsome and seductive, turned a copy of verses with the best of gentlemen, but was particularly distinguished by the art with which he purveyed little dramas for the amateur stage, then so much in fashion in France. Somebody said of him, when he was famous as the laureate of the cats, that he had risen in life by never scratching, by always having velvet paws, and by never putting up his back, even when he was startled. Voltaire called him "my very dear Sylph," and he was the ideal of all that was noiseless, graceful, good-humoured, and well-bred. He slipped unobtrusively into the French Academy, and lived to be eighty-three, dying at last, like Anacreon, in the midst of music and dances and fair nymphs of the Opera, affecting to be a sad old rogue to the very last.

This book on Cats, the only one by which he is now remembered, was the sole production of his lifetime which cost him any annoyance. He was forty years of age when it appeared, and the subject was considered a little frivolous, even for such a *petit conteur* as Moncrif. People continued to tease him about it, and the only rough thing he ever did was the result of one such twitting. The poet Roy made an epigram about "cats" and "rats," in execrable taste, no doubt; this stung our Sylph to such an excess that he waited outside the Palais Royal and beat Roy with a stick when he came out. The poet was, perhaps, not much hurt; at all events, he had the presence of mind to retort, "Patte de velours, patte de velours, Minon-minet!" It was six years after this that Moncrif was elected into the French Academy, and then the shower of epigrams broke out again. He wished to be made historiographer; "Oh, nonsense," the wits cried, "he must mean historiogriffe" and they invited him, on nights when the Academy met, to climb on to the roof and miau from the chimneypots. He had the weakness to apologise for his charming book, and to withdraw it from circulation. His pastoral tales and heroic ballets, his *Zelindors* and *Zeloides* and *Erosines*, which to us seem utterly vapid and frivolous, never gave him a moment's uneasiness. His crumpled rose-leaf was the book by which his name lives in literature.

The book of cats is written in the form of eleven letters to Madame la Marquise de B----. The anonymous author represents himself as too much excited to sleep, after an evening spent in a fashionable house, where the company was abusing cats. He was unsupported; where was the Marquise, who would have brought a thousand arguments to his assistance, founded on her own experience of virtuous pussies? Instead of going to bed he will sit up and indite the panegyric of the feline race. He is still sore at the prejudice and injustice of the people he has just left. It culminated in the conduct of a lady who declared that cats were poison, and who, "when pussy appeared in the room, had the presence of mind to faint." These people had rallied him on the absurdity of his enthusiasm; but, as he says, the Marquise well knows, "how many women have a passion for cats, and how many men are women in this respect."

So he starts away on his dissertation, with all its elegant pedantry, its paradoxical wit, its genuine touches of observation and its constant sparkle of anecdote. He is troubled to account for the existence of the cat. An Ottoman legend relates that when the animals were in the Ark, Noah gave the lion a great box on the ear, which made him sneeze, and produce a cat out his nose. But the author questions this origin, and is more inclined to agree with a Turkish Minister of Religion, sometime Ambassador to France, that the ape, "weary of a sedentary life" in the Ark, paid his attentions to a very agreeable young lioness, whose infidelities resulted in the birth of a Tom-cat and a Puss-cat, and that these, combining the qualities of their parents, spread through the Ark *un esprit de coquetterie*--which lasted during the whole of the sojourn there. Moncrif has no difficulty in showing that the East has always been devoted to cats, and he tells the story of Mahomet, who, being consulted one day on a point of piety, preferred to cut off his sleeve, on which his favourite pussy was asleep, rather than wake her violently by rising.

From the French poets, Moncrif collects a good many curious tributes to the "harmless, necessary cat." I am seized with an ambition to put some fragments of these into English verse. Most of them are highly complimentary. It is true that Ronsard was one of those who could not appreciate a "matou." He sang or said:

There is no man now living anywhere
Who hates cats with a deeper hate than I;
I hate their eyes, their heads, the way they stare,
And when I see one come, I turn and fly.

But among the *precieuses* of the seventeenth century there was much more appreciation. Mme. Deshoulieres wrote a whole series of songs and couplets about her cat, Grisette. In a letter to her husband, referring to the attentions she herself receives from admirers, she adds:

Deshoulieres cares not for the smart

Her bright eyes cause, disdainful hussy,

But, like a mouse, her idle heart

Is captured by a pussy.

Much better than these is the sonnet on the cat of the Duchess of Lesdiguieres, with its admirable line:

Chatte pour tout le monde, et pour les chats tigresse.

A fugitive epistle by Scarron, delightfully turned, is too long to be quoted here, nor can I pause to cite the rondeau which the Duchess of Maine addressed to her favourite. But she supplemented it as follows:

My pretty puss, my solace and delight,

To celebrate thy loveliness aright

I ought to call to life the bard who sung

Of Lesbia's sparrow with so sweet a tongue;

But 'tis in vain to summon here to me

So famous a dead personage as he,

And you must take contentedly to-day

This poor rondeau that Cupid wafts your way.

When this cat died the Duchess was too much affected to write its epitaph herself, and accordingly it was done for her, in the following style, by La Mothe le Vayer, the author of the **Dialogues**:

Puss passer-by, within this simple tomb

Lies one whose life fell Atropos hath shred;

The happiest cat on earth hath heard her doom,

And sleeps for ever in a marble bed.

Alas! what long delicious days I've seen!

O cats of Egypt, my illustrious sires,

You who on altars, bound with garlands green,

Have melted hearts, and kindled fond desires,--

Hymns in your praise were paid, and offerings too,

But I'm not jealous of those rights divine.

Since Ludovisa loved me, close and true,
Your ancient glory was less proud than mine.
To live a simple pussy by her side
Was nobler far than to be deified.

To these and other tributes Moncrif adds idyls and romances of his own, while regretting that it never occurred to Theocritus to write a ***bergerie de chats***. He tells stories of blameless pussies beloved by Fontanelle and La Fontaine, and quotes Marot in praise of "the green-eyed Venus." But he tears himself away at last from all these historical reminiscences, and in his eleventh letter he deals with cats as they are. We hasten as lightly as possible over a story of the disinterestedness of a feline Heloise, which is too pathetic for a nineteenth-century ear. But we may repeat the touching anecdote of Bayle's friend, Mlle. Dupuy. This lady excelled to a surprising degree in playing the harp, and she attributed her excellence in this accomplishment to her cat, whose critical taste was only equalled by his close attention to Mlle. Dupuy's performance. She felt that she owed so much to this cat, under whose care her reputation for skill on the harp had become universal, that when she died she left him, in her will, one agreeable house in town and another in the country. To this bequest she added a revenue sufficient to supply all the requirements of a well-bred tom-cat, and at the same time she left pensions to certain persons whose duty it should be to wait upon him. Her ignoble family contested the will, and there was a long suit. Moncrif gives a handsome double-plate illustration of this incident. Mlle. Dupuy, sadly wasted by illness, is seen in bed, with her cat in her arms, dictating her will to the family lawyer in a periwig; her physician is also present.

This leads me to speak of the illustrations to ***Les Chats***, which greatly add to its value. They were engraved by Otten from original drawings by Coypel. In another edition the same drawings are engraved by Count Caylus. Some of them are of a charming absurdity. One, a double plate, represents a tragedy acted by cats on the roof of a fashionable house. The actors are tricked out in the most magnificent feathers and furbelows, but the audience consists of common cats. Cupid sits above, with his bow and fluttering wings. Another plate shows the mausoleum of the Duchess of Lesdiguieres' cat, with a marble pussy of heroic size, upon a marble pillow, in a grove of poplars. Another is a medal to "Chat Noir premier, ne en 1725," with the proud inscription, "Knowing to whom I belong, I am aware of my value."

The profile within is that of as haughty a tom as ever shook out his whiskers in a lady's boudoir.

SMART'S POEMS

POEMS ON SEVERAL OCCASIONS. *By Christopher Smart, A.M., Fellow of Pembroke-Hall, Cambridge. London: Printed for the Author, by W. Strahan; And sold by J. Newbery, at the Bible and Sun, in St. Paul's Churchyard. MDC-CLII.*

The third section of Robert Browning's *Parleyings with certain People of Importance in their Day* drew attention to a Cambridge poet of whom little had hitherto been known, Christopher Smart, once fellow of Pembroke College. It may be interesting, therefore, to supply some sketch of the events of his life, and of the particular poem which Browning has aptly compared to a gorgeous chapel lying perdue in a dull old commonplace mansion. No one can afford to be entirely indifferent to the author of verses which one of the greatest of modern writers has declared to be unequalled of their kind between Milton and Keats.

What has hitherto been known of the facts of Smart's life has been founded on the anonymous biography prefixed to the two-volume Reading edition of his works, published in 1791. The copy of this edition in Trinity Library belonged to Dr. Farmer, and contains these words in his handwriting: "From the Editor, Francis Newbery, Esq.; the Life by Mr. Hunter." As this Newbery was the son of Smart's half-brother-in-law and literary employer, it may be taken for granted that the information given in these volumes is authoritative. We may therefore believe it to be correct that Smart was born (as he himself tells us, in The Hop Garden) at Shipbourne, in Kent, on the 11th of April 1722, that his father was steward to the nobleman who afterwards became Earl of Darlington, and that he was "discerned and patronised" by the Duchess of Cleveland. This great lady, we are left in doubt for what reason, carried her complaisance so far as to allow the future poet L40 a year until her death. In a painfully fulsome ode to another member of the Raby Castle family, Smart records the generosity of the dead in order to stimulate that of the living, and oddly remarks that dignity itself restrains

By condescension's silken reins,

While you the lowly Muse upraise.

Smart passed, already "an infant bard," from what he calls "the splendour in retreat" of Raby Castle, to Durham School, and in his eighteenth year was admitted of Pembroke Hall, October 30, 1739. His biographer expressly states that his allowance from home was scanty, and that his chief dependence, until he derived an income from his college, was on the bounty of the Duchess of Cleveland.

From this point I am able to supply a certain amount of information with regard to the poet's college life which is entirely new, and which is not, I think, without interest. My friend Mr. R.A. Neil has been so kind as to admit me to the Treasury at Pembroke, and in his company I have had the advantage of searching the contemporary records of the college. What we were lucky enough to discover may here be briefly summarised. The earliest mention of Smart is dated 1740, and refers to the rooms assigned to him as an undergraduate. In January 1743, we find him taking his B.A., and in July of the same year he is elected scholar. As is correctly stated in his Life, he became a fellow of Pembroke on the 3rd of July 1745. That he showed no indication as yet of that disturbance of brain and instability of character which so painfully distinguished him a little later on, is proved by the fact that on the 10th of October 1745, Smart was chosen to be Praelector in Philosophy, and Keeper of the Common Chest. In 1746 he was re-elected to those offices, and also made Praelector in Rhetoric. In 1747 he was not chosen to hold any such college situations, no doubt from the growing extravagance of his conduct.

In November 1747, Smart was in parlous case. Gray complains of his "lies, impertinence and ingratitude," and describes him as confined to his room, lest his creditors should snap him up. He gives a melancholy impression of Smart's moral and physical state, but hastens to add "not that I, nor any other mortal, pity him." The records of the Treasury at Pembroke supply evidence that the members of the college now made a great effort to restore one of whose talents it is certain they were proud. In 1748 we find Smart proposed for catechist, a proof that he had, at all events for the moment, turned over a new leaf. Probably, but for fresh relapses, he would now have taken orders. His allusions to college life are singularly ungracious. He calls Pembroke this servile cell,

Where discipline and dulness dwell,

and commiserates a captive eagle as being doomed in the college courts to watch

scholastic pride

Take his precise, pedantic stride;

words which painfully remind us of Gray's reported manner of enjoying a constitutional. It is certain that there was considerable friction between these two men of genius, and Gray roundly prophesied that Smart would find his way to gaol or to Bedlam. Both alternatives of this prediction were fulfilled, and in October, 1751, Gray curtly remarks: "Smart sets out for Bedlam." Of this event we find curious evidence in the Treasury. "October 12, 1751--Ordered that Mr. Smart, being obliged to be absent, there will be allowed him in lieu of commons for the year ended Michaelmas, 1751, the sum of L10." There can be little question that Smart's conduct and condition became more and more unsatisfactory. This particular visit to a madhouse was probably brief, but it was possibly not the first and was soon repeated; for in 1749 and 1752 there are similar entries recording the fact that "Mr. Smart, being obliged to be absent," certain allowances were paid by the college "in consideration of his circumstances." The most curious discovery, however, which we have been able to make is recorded in the following entry:

"Nov. 27, 1753.--Ordered that the dividend assigned to Mr. Smart be deposited in the Treasury till the Society be satisfied that he has a right to the same; it being credibly reported that he has been married for some time, and that notice be sent to Mr. Smart of his dividend being detained."

As a matter of fact, Smart was by this time married to a relative of Newbery, the publisher, for whom he was doing hack work in London. He had, however, formed the habit of writing the Seatonian prize poem, which he had already gained four times, in 1750, 1751, 1752, and 1753. He seems to have clutched at the distinction which he brought on his college by these poems as the last straw by which to keep his fellowship, and, singular to say, he must have succeeded; for on the 16th of January 1754, this order was recorded:

"That Mr. Smart have leave to keep his name in the college books without any expense, so long as he continues to write for the premium left by Mr. Seaton."

How long this inexpensive indulgence lasted does not seem to be known. Smart gained the Seatonian prize in 1755, having apparently failed in 1754, and then appears no more in Pembroke records.

The circumstance of his having made Cambridge too hot to hold him seems to have pulled Smart's loose faculties together. The next five years were probably the sanest and the busiest in his life. He had collected his scattered odes and ballads, and published them, with his ambitious georgic, *The Hop Garden*, in the handsome quarto before us. Among the seven hundred subscribers to this venture we find "Mr. Voltaire, historiographer of France," and M. Roubilliac, the great statuary, besides such English celebrities as Gray, Collins, Richardson, Savage, Charles Avison, Garrick, and Mason. The kind reception of this work awakened in the poet an inordinate vanity, which found expression, in 1753, in that extraordinary effusion, *The Hilliad*, an attempt to preserve Dr. John Hill in such amber as Pope held at the command of his satiric passion. But these efforts, and an annual Seatonian, were ill adapted to support a poet who had recently appended a wife and family to a phenomenal appetite for strong waters, and who, moreover, had just been deprived of his stipend as a fellow. Smart descended into Grub Street, and bound himself over, hand and foot, to be the serf of such men as the publisher Newbery, who was none the milder master for being his relative. It was not long after, doubtless, that Smart fell lower still, and let himself out on a lease for ninety-nine years, to toil for a set pittance in the garrets of Gardner's shop; and it was about this time, 1754, that the Rev. T. Tyers was introduced to Smart by a friend who had more sympathy with his frailties than Gray had, namely, Dr. Samuel Johnson.

After a world of vicissitudes, which are very uncomfortable reading, about 1761 Smart became violently insane once more and was shut up again in Bedlam. Dr. Johnson, commenting on this period of the poet's life, told Dr. Burney that Smart grew fat when he was in the madhouse, where he dug in the garden, and Johnson added: "I did not think he ought to be shut up. His infirmities were not noxious to society. He insisted on people praying with him; and I'd as lief pray with Kit Smart as with any one else. Another charge was that he did not love clean linen; and I have no passion for it." When Boswell paid Johnson his memorable first visit in 1763, Smart had recently been released from Bedlam, and Johnson naturally spoke of him. He said: "My poor friend Smart showed the disturbance of his mind by falling upon his knees and saying his prayers in the street, or in any other un- usual place." Gray about the same time reports that money is being collected to help "poor Smart," not for the first time, since in January 1759, Gray had written: "Poor Smart is not dead, as was said, and *Merope* is acted for his benefit this week," with the *Guardian*, a farce which Garrick had kindly composed for that occasion.

It was in 1763, immediately after Smart's release, that the now famous ***Song to David*** was published. A long and interesting letter in the correspondence of Hawkesworth, dated October 1764, gives a pleasant idea of Smart restored to cheer- fulness and placed "with very decent people in a house, most delightfully situated, with a terrace that overlooks St. James's Park." But this relief was only temporary; Smart fell back presently into drunkenness and debt, and was happily relieved by death in 1770, in his forty-eighth year, at the close of a career as melancholy as any recorded in the chronicles of literature.

Save for one single lyric, that glows with all the flush and bloom of Eden, Smart would take but a poor place on the English Parnassus. His odes and ballads, his psalms and satires, his masques and his georgics, are not bad, but they are medio- cre. Here and there the very careful reader may come across lines and phrases that display the concealed author of the ***Song to David***, such as the following, from an excessively tiresome ode to Dr. Webster:

When Israel's host, with all their stores,   Passed through the ruby-tinc- tured crystal shores, The wilderness of waters and of land.

But these are rare. His odes are founded upon those of Gray, and the best that can be said of them is that if they do not quite rise to the frozen elegance of Aken- side, they seldom sink to the flaccidity of Mason. Never, for one consecutive stanza or stroke, do they approach Collins or Gray in delicacy or power. But the ***Song to David***--the lyric in 516 lines which Smart is so absurdly fabled to have scratched with a key on the white-washed walls of his cell--this was a portent of beauty and originality. Strange to say, it was utterly neglected when it appeared, and the editor of the 1791 edition of Smart's works expressly omitted to print it on the ground that it bore too many "melancholy proofs of the estrangement of Smart's mind" to be fit for republication. It became rare to the very verge of extinction, and is now scarcely to be found in its entirety save in a pretty reprint of 1819, itself now rare, due to the piety of a Rev. R. Harvey.

It is obvious that Smart's contemporaries and immediate successors looked upon the ***Song to David*** as the work of a hopelessly deranged person. In 1763 poetry had to be very sane indeed to be attended to. The year preceding had welcomed the ***Shipwreck*** of Falconer, the year to follow would welcome Goldsmith's ***Traveller*** and Grainger's ***Sugar Cane***, works of various merit, but all eminently sane. In 1763 Shenstone was dying and Rogers was being born. The tidy, spruce, and discreet poetry of the eighteenth century was passing into its final and most pronounced stage. The ***Song to David***, with its bold mention of unfamiliar things, its warm and highly-coloured phraseology, its daring adjectives and unexampled adverbs, was an outrage upon taste, and one which was best accounted for by the tap of the forefinger on the forehead. No doubt the poem presented and still may present legitimate difficulties. Here, for instance, is a stanza which it is not for those who run to read:

> Increasing days their reign exalt,
> Nor in the pink and mottled vault
> The opposing spirits tilt;
> And, by the coasting reader spy'd,
> The silverlings and crusions glide
> For Adoration gilt.

This is charming; but if it were in one of the tongues of the heathen we should get Dr. Verrall to explain it away. Poor Mr. Harvey, the editor of 1819, being hopelessly puzzled by "silverlings," the only dictionary meaning of which is "shekels," explained "crusions" to be some other kind of money, from [Greek: krousis]. But "crusions" are golden carp, and when I was a child the Devonshire fishermen used to call the long white fish with argent stripes (whose proper name, I think, is the launce) a silverling. The "coasting reader" is the courteous reader when walking along the coast, and what he sees are silver fish and gold fish, adoring the Lord by the beauty of their scales. The ***Song to David*** is cryptic to a very high degree, but I think there are no lines in it which patient reflection will not solve. On every page are stanzas the verbal splendour of which no lover of poetry will question, and lines which will always, to me at least, retain an echo of that gusto with which I have heard Mr. Browning's strong voice recite them:

    The wealthy crops of whitening rice
'Mongst thyine woods and groves of spice,
For Adoration grow;
And, marshall'd in the fenced land,
The peaches and pomegranates stand,
Where wild carnations blow.
   The laurels with the winter strive;
The crocus burnishes alive
Upon the snow-clad earth;

   For Adoration ripening canes
And cocoa's purest milk detains
The westering pilgrim's staff;
Where rain in, clasping boughs inclos'd,
And vines with oranges dispos'd,
Embower the social laugh.
   For Adoration, beyond match,
The scholar bulfinch aims to catch
The soft flute's ivory touch;
And, careless on the hazle spray,
The daring redbreast keeps at bay
The damsel's greedy clutch.

To quote at further length from so fascinating, so divine a poem, would be "purpling too much my mere grey argument." Browning's praise ought to send every one to the original. But here is one more stanza that I cannot resist copying, because it seems so pathetically applicable to Smart himself as a man, and to the one exquisite poem which was "the more than Abishag of his age":

   His muse, bright angel of his verse,
Gives balm for all the thorns that pierce,
For all the pangs that rage;
Blest light, still gaining on the gloom,
The more than Michal of his bloom,

The Abishag of his age.

POMPEY THE LITTLE

THE HISTORY OF POMPEY THE LITTLE; *or, the Life and Adventures of a Lap-Dog. London: Printed for M. Cooper, at the Globe in Paternoster Row, MDCCLI*.

In February 1751 the town, which had been suffering from rather a dreary spell since the acceptable publication of *Tom Jones*, was refreshed and enlivened by the simultaneous issue of two delightfully scandalous productions, eminently well adapted to occupy the polite conversation of ladies at drums and at the card-table. Of these one was *The Memoirs of a Lady of Quality*, so oddly foisted by Smollett into the third volume of his *Peregrine Pickle*. This was recognised at once as being the work of the frail and adventurous Lady Vane, about whom so many strange stories were already current in society. The other puzzled the gossips much longer, and it seems to have been the poet Gray who first discovered the authorship of *Pompey the Little*. Gray wrote to tell Horace Walpole who had written the anonymous book that everybody was talking about, adding that he had discovered the secret through the author's own carelessness, three of the characters being taken from a comedy shown him by a young clergyman at Magdalen College, Cambridge. This was the Rev. Francis Coventry, then some twenty-five years of age. The discovery of the authorship made Coventry a nine-days' hero, while his book went into a multitude of editions. It was one of the most successful *jeux d'esprit* of the eighteenth century.

The copy of the first edition of *Pompey the Little*, which lies before me, contains an excellent impression of the frontispiece by Louis Boitard, the fashionable engraver-designer, whose print of the Ranelagh Rotunda is so much sought after by amateurs. It represents a curtain drawn aside to reveal a velvet cushion, on which sits a graceful little Italian lap-dog with pendant silky ears and sleek sides spotted like the pard. This is Pompey the Little, whose life and adventures the book proceeds to recount. "*Pompey*, the son of *Julio* and *Phyllis*, was born A.D. 1735, at *Bologna* in *Italy*, a place famous for lap-dogs and sausages." At an early age he was carried away from the boudoir of his Italian mistress by Hillario, an English gentleman illustrious for his gallantries, who brought him to London. The rest of the history is really a chain of social episodes, each closed by the incident that Pompey becomes the property of some fresh person. In this way we find ourselves in a dozen successive scenes, each strongly contrasted with the others. It is the art of the author that he knows exactly how much to tell us without wearying our attention, and is able to make the transition to the next scene a plausible one.

There is low life as well as high life in *Pompey the Little*, sketches after Hogarth, no less than studies *a la* Watteau. But the high life is by far the better described. Francis Coventry was the cousin of the Earl of that name, he who married the beautiful and silly Maria Gunning. When he painted the ladies of quality at their routs and drums, masquerades, and hurly-burlies, he knew what he was talking about, for this was the life he himself led, when he was not at college. Even at Cambridge, he was under the dazzling influence of his famous and fashionable cousin, Henry Coventry, fellow of the same college of Magdalen, author of the polite *Philemonto Hydaspes* dialogues, and the latest person who dressed well in the University. The embroidered coats of Henry Coventry, stiff with gold lace, his "most prominent Roman nose" and air of being much a gentleman, were not lost on the younger member of the family, who seems to paint him slyly in his portrait of Mr. Williams.

The great charm of *Pompey the Little* to contemporaries was, of course, the fact that it was supposed to be a *roman a clef*. The Countess of Bute hastened to send out a copy of it to her mother in Italy, and Lady Mary Wortley Montagu did not hesitate to discover the likenesses of various dear friends of hers. She found it impossible to go to bed till she had finished it. She was charmed, and she tells Lady Bute, what the curious may now read with great satisfaction, that it was "a real and exact representation of life, as it is now acted in London." What is odd is that Lady Mary identified, with absolute complacency, the portrait of herself, as Mrs. Qualmsick, that hysterical lady with whom "it was not unusual for her to fancy herself a Glass bottle, a Tea-pot, a Hay-rick, or a Field of Turnips." Instead of being angry, Lady Mary screamed with laughter at the satire of her own whimsies, of how "Red was too glaring for her eyes; Green put her in Mind of Willows, and made her melancholic; Blue remembered her of her dear Sister, who had died ten Years before in a blue Bed." In fact, all this fun seems, for the moment at least, to have cured the original Mrs. Qualmsick of her whimsies, and her remarks on ***Pompey the Little*** are so good-natured that we may well forgive her for the pleasure with which she recognised Lady Townshend in Lady Tempest and the Countess of Orford in the pedantic and deistical Lady Sophister, who rates the physicians for their theology, and will not be bled by any man who accepts the doctrine of the immortality of the soul.

Coventry's romance does not deserve the entire neglect into which it has fallen. It is sprightly and graceful from the first page to the last. Not written, indeed, by a man of genius, it is yet the work of a very refined observer, who had been modern enough to catch the tone of the new school of novelists. The writer owes much to Fielding, who yet does not escape without a flap from one of Pompey's silken ears. Coventry's manner may be best exemplified by one of his own bright passages of satire. This notion of a man of quality, that no place can be full that is not crowded with people of fashion, is not new, but it is deliciously expressed. Aurora has come back from Bath, and assures the Count that she has had a pleasant season there:

"'You amaze me," cries the Count; 'Impossible, Madam! How can it be, Ladies? I had Letters from Lord ***Monkeyman*** and Lady ***Betty Scornful*** assuring me that, except yourselves, there were not three human Creatures in the Place. Let me see, I have Lady ***Betty's*** Letter in my Pocket, I believe, at this Moment. Oh no, upon Recollection, I put it this morning into my Cabinet, where I preserve all my Letters of Quality.' ***Aurora***, smothering a Laugh as well as she could, said she was extremely obliged to Lord ***Monkeyman*** and Lady ***Betty***, for vouchsafing to rank her and her Sister in the Catalogue of human Beings. 'But, surely,' added she, 'they must have been asleep, both of them, when they wrote their Letters; for the ***Bath*** was extremely full,' 'Full!' cries the Count, interrupting her; "Oh, Madam, that is very possible, and yet there might be no Company--that is, none of us; Nobody that one knows. For as to all the Tramontanes that come by the cross Post, we never reckon them as anything but Monsters in human Shape, that serve to fill up the Stage of Life, like Cyphers in a play. For Instance, you often see an awkward Girl, who has sewed a Tail to a Gown, and pinned two Lappits to a Night-cap, come running headlong into the Rooms with a wild, frosty Face, as if she was just come from feeding Poultry in her Father's Chicken-Yard. Or you see a Booby Squire, with a

Head resembling a Stone ball over a Gate-post. Now, it would be the most ridiculous Thing in Life to call such People Company. 'Tis the Want of Titles, and not the Want of Faces, that makes a Place empty.'"

There are indications, which I think have escaped the notice of Goldsmith's editors, that the author of the *Citizen of the World* condescended to take some of his ideas from *Pompey the Little*. In Count Tag, the impoverished little fop who fancies himself a man of quality, and who begs pardon of people who accost him in the Park--"but really, Lady Betty or Lady Mary is just entering the Mall,"--we have the direct prototype of Beau Tibbs; while Mr. Rhymer, the starving poet, whose furniture consists of "the first Act of a Comedy, a Pair of yellow Stays, two political Pamphlets, a plate of Bread-and-butter, three dirty Night-caps, and a Volume of Miscellany Poems," is a figure wonderfully like that of Goldsmith himself, as Dr. Percy found him eight years later, in that "wretched, dirty room," at the top of Breakneck Steps, Green Arbour Court. The whole conception of that Dickens-like scene, in which it is described how Lady Frippery had a drum in spite of all local difficulties, is much more in the humour of Goldsmith than in that of any of Coventry's immediate contemporaries.

Strangely enough, in spite of the great success of his one book, the author of *Pompey the Little* never tried to repeat it. He became perpetual curate of Edgware, and died in the neighbouring village of Stanmore Parva a few years after the publication of his solitary book; I have, however, searched the registers of that parish in vain for any record of the fact. Francis Coventry had gifts of wit and picturesqueness which deserved a better fate than to amuse a few dissipated women over their citron-waters, and then to be forgotten.

THE LIFE OF JOHN BUNCLE

THE LIFE OF JOHN BUNCLE, ESQ., *containing various observations and reflections made in several parts of the world; and many extraordinary relations. London: Printed for J. Noon, at the White Hart in Cheapside, near the Poultry, MDCCLVI.*

[*Vol. II. London: Printed for J. Johnson and B. Davenport, at the Globe, in*

Pater Noster Row, MDCCLXVI.]

In the year 1756, there resided in the Barbican, where the great John Milton had lived before him, a funny elderly personage called Mr. Thomas Amory, of whom not nearly so much is recorded as the lovers of literary anecdote would like to possess. He was sixty-five years of age; he was an Irish gentleman of means, and he was an ardent Unitarian. Some unkind people have suggested that he was out of his mind, and he had, it is certain, many peculiarities. One was, that he never left his house, or ventured into the streets, save "like a but, in the dusk of the evening." He was, in short, what is called a "crank," and he gloried in his eccentricity. He desired that it might be written on his tombstone, "Here lies an Odd Man." For sixty years he had made no effort to attract popular attention, but in 1755 he had published a sort of romance, called ***Memoirs of Several Ladies of Great Britain***, and now he succeeded it by the truly extraordinary work, the name of which stands at the head of this article. Ten years later there would appear another volume of ***John Buncle***, and then Amory disappeared again. All we know is, that he died in 1788, at the very respectable age of ninety-seven. So little is known about him, so successfully did he hide "like a but" through the dusk of nearly a century, that we may be glad to eke out the scanty information given above by a passage of autobiography from the preface of the book before us:

"I was born in London, and carried an infant to Ireland, where I learned the Irish language, and became intimately acquainted with its original inhabitants. I was not only a lover of books from the time I could spell them to this hour, but read with an extraordinary pleasure, before I was twenty, the works of several of the Fathers, and all the old romances; which tinged my ideas with a certain piety and extravagance that rendered my virtues as well as my imperfections particularly mine.... The dull, the formal, and the visionary, the hard-honest man, and the poor-liver, are a people I have had no connection with; but have always kept company with the polite, the generous, the lively, the rational, and the brightest freethinkers of this age. Besides all this, I was in the days of my youth, one of the most active men in the world at every exercise; and to a degree of rashness, often venturesome, when there was no necessity for running any hazards; ***in diebus illis***, I have descended headforemost, from a high cliff into the ocean, to swim, when I could, and ought, to have gone off a rock not a yard from the surface of the deep. I have swam near a mile and a half out in the sea to a ship that lay off, gone on board, got clothes from the mate of the vessel, and proceeded with them to the next port; while my companion I left on the beach concluded me drowned, and related my sad fate in the town. I have taken a cool thrust over a bottle, without the least animosity on either side, but both of us depending on our skill in the small sword for preservation from mischief. Such things as these I now call wrong."

If this is not a person of whom we would like to know more, I know not what the romance of biography is. Thomas Amory's life must have been a streak of crimson on the grey surface of the eighteenth century. It is really a misfortune that the red is almost all washed off.

No odder book than **John Buncle** was published in England throughout the long life of Amory. Romances there were, like **Gulliver's Travels** and **Peter Wilkins**, in which the incidents were much more incredible, but there was no supposition that these would be treated as real history. The curious feature of **John Buncle** is that the story is told with the strictest attention to realism and detail, and yet is embroidered all over with the impossible. There can be no doubt that Amory, who belonged to an older school, was affected by the form of the new novels which were the fashion in 1756. He wished to be as particular as Mr. Richardson, as manly as Captain Fielding, as breezy and vigorous as Dr. Smollett, the three new writers who were all the talk of the town. But there was a twist in his brain which made his pictures of real life appear like scenes looked at through flawed glass.

The memoirs of John Buncle take the form of an autobiography, and there has been much discussion as to how much is, and how much is not, the personal history of Amory. I confess I cannot see why we should not suppose all of it to be invented, although it certainly is odd to relate anecdotes and impressions of Dr. Swift, *a propos* of nothing at all, unless they formed part of the author's experience. For one thing, the hero is represented as being born about thirteen years later than Amory was--if, indeed, we possess the true date of our worthy's birth. Buncle goes to college and becomes an earnest Unitarian. The incidents of his life are all intellectual, until one "glorious first of August," when he sallies forth from college with his gun and dog, and after four hours' walk discovers that he has lost his way. He is in the midst of splendid mountain scenery--which leads us to wonder at which English University he was studying--and descends through woody ravines and cliffs that overhang torrents, till he suddenly comes in sight of a "little harmonic building that had every charm and proportion architecture could give it." Finding one of the garden doors open, and being very hungry, the adventurous Buncle strolls in, and finds himself in "a grotto or shell-house, in which a politeness of fancy had produced and blended the greatest beauties of nature and decoration." (There are more grottoes in the pages of Amory than exist in the whole of the British Islands.) This shell-house opened into a library, and in the library a beauteous object was sitting and reading. She was studying a Hebrew Bible, and making philological notes on a small desk. She raised her eyes and approached the stranger, "to know who I wanted" (for Buncle's style, though picturesque, is not always grammatically irreproachable.)

Before he could answer, a venerable gentleman was at his side, to whom the young sportsman confessed that he was dying of hunger and had lost his way. Mr. Noel, a patriarchal widower of vast wealth, was inhabiting this mansion in the sole company of his only daughter, the lovely being just referred to. Mr. Buncle was immediately "stiffened by enchantment" at the beauty of Miss Harriot Noel, and could not be induced to leave when he had eaten his breakfast. This difficulty was removed by the old gentleman asking him to stay to dinner, until the time of which meal Miss Noel should entertain him. At about 10 A.M. Mr. Buncle offers his hand to the astonished Miss Noel, who, with great propriety, bids him recollect that he is an entire stranger to her. They then have a long conversation about the Chaldeans, and the "primaevity" of the Hebrew language, and the extraordinary longevity of the Antediluvians; at the close of which (circa 11.15 A.M.) Buncle proposes again. "You force me to smile (the illustrious Miss Noel replied), and oblige me to call you an odd compound of a man," and to distract his thoughts, she takes him round her famous grotto. The conversation, all repeated at length, turns on conchology and on the philosophy of Epictetus until it is time for dinner, when Mr. Noel and young Buncle drink a bottle of old Alicant, and discuss the gallery of Verres and the poetry of Catullus. Left alone at last, Buncle still does not go away, but at 5 P.M. proposes for the third time, "over a pot of tea." Miss Noel says that the conversation will have to take some other turn, or she must leave the room. They therefore immediately "consider the miracle at Babel," and the argument of Hutchinson on the Hebrew word ***Shephah***, until, while Miss Noel is in the very act of explaining that "the Aramitish was the customary language of the line of Shem," young Buncle (circa

7.30) "could not help snatching this beauty to my arms, and without thinking what I did, impressed on her balmy mouth half a dozen kisses. This was wrong, and gave offence," but then papa returning, the trio sat down peacefully to cribbage and a little music. Of course Miss Noel is ultimately won, and this is a very fair specimen of the conduct of the book.

A fortnight before the marriage, however, "the small-pox steps in, and in seven days' time reduced the finest human frame in the universe to the most hideous and offensive block," and Miss Harriot Noel dies. If this dismal occurrence is rather abruptly introduced, it is because Buncle has to be betrothed, in succession, to six other lively and delicious young females, all of them beautiful, all of them learned, and all of them earnestly convinced Unitarians. If they did not rapidly die off, how could they be seven? Buncle mourns the decease of each, and then hastily forms an equally violent attachment to another. It must be admitted that he is a sad wife-waster. Azora is one of the most delightful of these deciduous loves. She "had an amazing collection of the most rational philosophical ideas, and she delivered them in the most pleasing dress." She resided in a grotto within a romantic dale in York-shire, in a "little female republic" of one hundred souls, all of them "straight, clean, handsome girls." In this glen there is only one man, and he a fossil. Miss Melmoth, who would discuss the ***paulo-post futurum*** of a Greek verb with the utmost care and politeness, and had studied "the Minerva of Sanctius and Hickes' Northern Thesaurus," was another nice young lady, though rather free in her manner with gentlemen. But they all die, sacrificed to the insatiable fate of Buncle.

Here the reader may like to enjoy a sample of Buncle as a philosopher. It is a characteristic passage:

"Such was the soliloquy I spoke, as I gazed on the skeleton of John Orton; and just as I had ended, the boys brought in the wild turkey, which they had very inge-niously roasted, and with some of Mrs. Burcot's fine ale and bread, I had an excel-lent supper. The bones of the penitent Orton I removed to a hole I had ordered my lad to dig for them; the skull excepted, which I kept, and still keep on my table for a ***memento mori***; and that I may never forget the good lesson which the percipient who once resided in it had given. It is often the subject of my meditation. When I am alone of an evening, in my closet, which is often my case, I have the skull of John Orton before me, and as I smoke a philosophic pipe, with my eyes fastened on it, I learn more from the solemn object than I could from the most philosophical and laboured speculations. What a wild and hot head once--how cold and still now; poor skull, I say: and what was the end of all thy daring, frolics and gambols--thy licentiousness and impiety--a severe and bitter repentance. In piety and goodness John Orton found at last that happiness the world could not give him."

Hazlitt has said that "the soul of Rabelais passed into John Amory." His name was Thomas, not John, and there is very little that is Rabelaisian in his spirit. One sees what Hazlitt meant--the voluble and diffuse learning, the desultory thread of narration, the mixture of religion and animalism. But the resemblance is very superficial, and the parallel too complimentary to Amory. It is difficult to think of the soul of Rabelais in connection with a pedantic and uxorious Unitarian. To lovers of odd books, *John Buncle* will always have a genuine attraction. Its learning would have dazzled Dr. Primrose, and is put on in glittering spars and shells, like the ornaments of the many grottoes that it describes. It is diversified by descriptions of natural scenery, which are often exceedingly felicitous and original, and it is quickened by the human warmth and flush of the love passages, which, with all their quaintness, are extremely human. It is essentially a "healthy" book, as Charles Lamb, with such a startling result, assured the Scotchman. Amory was a fervid admirer of womankind, and he favoured a rare type, the learned lady who bears her learning lightly and can discuss "the quadrations of curvilinear spaces" without ceasing to be "a bouncing, dear, delightful girl," and adroit in the preparation of toast and chocolate. The style of the book is very careless and irregular, but rises in its best pages to an admirable picturesqueness.

BEAU NASH

THE LIFE OF RICHARD NASH, ESQ.; *late Master of the Ceremonies at Bath. Extracted principally from his Original Papers. The Second Edition. London: J. Newbery.* 1762.

There are cases, not known to every collector of books, where it is not the first which is the really desirable edition of a work, but the second. One of these rare examples of the exception which proves the rule is the second edition of Goldsmith's ***Life of Beau Nash***. Disappointment awaits him who possesses only the first; it is in the second that the best things originally appeared. The story is rather to be divined than told as history, but we can see pretty plainly how the lines of it must have run. In the early part of 1762, Oliver Goldsmith, at that time still undistinguished, but in the very act of blossoming into fame, received a commission of fourteen guineas to write for Newbery a life of the strange old beau, Mr. Nash, who had died in 1761. On the same day, which was March 5th, he gave a receipt to the publisher for three other publications, written or to be written, so that very probably it was not expected that he should immediately supply all the matter sold. In the summer he seems to have gone down to Bath on a short visit, and to have made friends with the Beau's executor, Mr. George Scott. It has even been said that he cultivated the Mayor and Aldermen of Bath with such success that they presented him with yet another fifteen guineas. But of this, in itself highly improbable, instance of municipal benefaction, the archives of the city yield no proof. At least Mr. Scott gave him access to Nash's papers, and with these he seems to have betaken himself back to London.

It is a heart-rending delusion and a cruel snare to be paid for your work before you accomplish it. As soon as once your work is finished you ought to be promptly paid; but to receive your lucre one minute before it is due, is to tempt Providence to make a Micawber of you. Goldsmith, of course, without any temptation being needed, was the very ideal Micawber of letters, and the result of paying him beforehand was that he had, simply, to be popped into the mill by force, and the copy ground out of him. It is evident that in the case of the first edition of the ***Life of Beau Nash***, the grinding process was too mercifully applied, and the book when it appeared was short measure. It has no dedication, no "advertisement," and very few notes, while it actually omits many of the best stories. The wise bibliophile, therefore, will eschew it, and will try to get the second edition issued a few weeks later in the same year, which Newbery evidently insisted that Goldsmith should send out to the public in proper order.

Goldsmith treats Nash with very much the same sort of indulgent and apologetic sympathy with which the late M. Barbey d'Aurevilly treats Brummell. He does not affect to think that the world calls for a full-length statue of such a fantastic hero; but he seems to claim leave to execute a statuette in terracotta for a cabinet of curiosities. From that point of view, as a queer object of **vertu**, as a specimen of the **bric-a-brac** of manners, both the one and the other, the King of Beaux and the Emperor of Dandies, are welcome to amateurs of the odd and the entertaining. At the head of Goldsmith's book stands a fine portrait of Nash, engraved by Anthony Walker, one of the best and rarest of early English line-engravers, after an oil-picture by William Hoare, presently to be one of the foundation-members of the Royal Academy, and now and throughout his long life the principal representative of the fine arts at Bath. Nash is here represented in his famous white hat--**galero albo**, as his epitaph has it; the ensign of his rule at Bath, the more than coronet of his social sway.

The breast of his handsome coat is copiously trimmed with rich lace, and his old, old eyes, with their wrinkles and their crow's feet, look demurely out from under an incredible wig, an umbrageous, deep-coloured ramilie of early youth. It is a wonderfully hard-featured, serious, fatuous face, and it lives for us under the delicate strokes of Anthony Walker's graver. The great Beau looks as he must have looked when the Duchess of Queensberry dared to appear at the Assembly House on a ball night with a white apron on. It is a pleasant story, and only told properly in our second edition. King Nash had issued an edict forbidding the wearing of aprons. The Duchess dared to disobey. Nash walked up to her and deftly snatched her apron from her, throwing it on to the back benches where the ladies' women sat. What a splendid moment! Imagine the excitement of all that fashionable company--the drawn battle between the Majesty of Etiquette and the Majesty of Beauty! The Beau remarked, with sublime calm, that "none but Abigails appeared in white aprons." The Duchess hesitated, felt that her ground had slipped from under her, gave way with the most admirable tact, and "with great good sense and humour, begged his **Majesty's** pardon,"

Aprons were not the only red rags to the bull of ceremony. He was quite as unflinching an enemy to top-boots. He had already banished swords from the assembly-room, because their clash frightened the ladies, and their scabbards tore people's dresses. But boots were not so easily banished. The country squires liked to ride into the city, and, leaving their horses at a stable, walk straight into the dignity of the minuet. Nash, who had a genius for propriety, saw how hateful this was, and determined to put a stop to it. He slew top-boots and aprons at the same time, and with the shaft of Apollo. He indited a poem on the occasion, and a very good example of satire by irony it is. It is short enough to quote entire:

FRONTINELLA'S INVITATION TO THE ASSEMBLY.

> Come, one and all,
> To Hoyden Hall,
> For there's th' Assembly to-night.
> None but prude fools
> Mind manners and rules,
> We Hoydens do decency slight.
> Come, Trollops and Slatterns,
> Cocked hats and white aprons,
> This best our modesty suits;
> For why should not we
> In dress be as free
> As Hogs-Norton squires in boots?

Why, indeed? But the Hogs-Norton squires, as is their wont, were not so easily pierced to the heart as the noble slatterns. Nash turned Aristophanes, and depicted on a little stage a play in which Mr. Punch, tinder very disgraceful circumstances, excused himself for wearing boots by quoting the practice of the pump-room beaux. This seems to have gone to the conscience of Hogs-Norton at last; but what really gave the death-blow to top-boots, as a part of evening dress, was the incident of Nash's going up to a gentleman, who had made his appearance in the ball-room in this unpardonable costume, and remarking, "bowing in an arch manner," that he appeared to have "forgotten his horse."

It had not been without labour and a long struggle that Nash had risen to this position of unquestioned authority at Bath. His majestic rule was the result of more than half a century of painstaking. He had been born far back in the seventeenth century, so far back that, incredible as it sounds, a love adventure of his early youth had supplied Vanbrugh, in 1695, with an episode for his comedy of *Aesop*. But after trying many forms of life, and weary of his own affluence, he came to Bath just at the moment when the fortunes of that ancient centre of social pleasure were at their lowest ebb. Queen Anne had been obliged to divert herself, in 1703, with a fiddle and a hautboy, and with country dances on the bowling-green. The lodgings were dingy and expensive, the pump-house had no director, the nobility had haughtily withdrawn from such vulgar entertainments as the city now alone afforded. The famous and choleric physician, Dr. Radcliffe, in revenge for some slight he had endured, had threatened to "throw a toad into King Bladud's Well," by writing a pamphlet against the medicinal efficacy of the waters.

The moment was critical; the greatness of Bath, which had been slowly declining since the days of Elizabeth, was threatened with extinction when Nash came to it, wealthy, idle, patient, with a genius for organisation, and in half a century he made it what he left it when he died in his eighty-ninth year, the most elegant and attractive of the smaller social resorts of Europe. Such a man, let us be certain, was not wholly ridiculous. There must have been something more in him than in a mere idol of the dandies, like Brummell, or a mere irresistible buck and lady-killer, like Lauzun. In these latter men the force is wholly destructive; they are animated by a feline vanity, a tiger-spirit of egotism. Against the story of Nash and the Duchess of Queensberry, so wholesome and humane, we put that frightful anecdote that Saint-Simon tells of Lauzun's getting the hand of another duchess under his high heel, and pirouetting on it to make the heel dig deeper into the flesh. In all the repertory of Nash's extravagances there is not one story of this kind, not one that reveals a wicked force. He was fatuous, but beneficent; silly, but neither cruel nor corrupt.

Goldsmith, in this second edition at least, has taken more pains with his life of Nash than he ever took again in a biography. His **Parnell**, his **Bolingbroke**, his **Voltaire**, are not worthy of his name and fame; not all the industry of annotators can ever make them more than they were at first--potboilers, turned out with no care or enthusiasm, and unconscientiously prepared. But this subtle figure of a Master of Ceremonial; this queer old presentment of a pump-room king, crowned with a white hat, waiting all day long in his best at the bow-window of the Smyrna Coffee-House to get a bow from that other, and alas! better accredited royalty, the Prince of Wales; this picture, of an old beau, with his toy-shop of gold snuff-boxes, his agate-rings, his senseless obelisk, his rattle of faded jokes and blunted stories--all this had something very attractive to Goldsmith both in its humour and its pathos; and he has left us, in his *Life of Nash*, a study which is far too little known, but which deserves to rank among the best-read productions of that infinitely sympathetic pen, which has bequeathed to posterity Mr. Tibbs and Moses Primrose and Tony Lumpkin.

THE NATURAL HISTORY OF SELBORNE

THE NATURAL HISTORY AND ANTIQUITIES OF SELBORNE, IN THE COUNTY OF SOUTHAMPTON; *with Engravings, and an Appendix. London: Printed by T. Bensley, for B. White and Son, at Horace's Head, Fleet Street. MDCCLXXXIX*.

It is not always the most confidently conducted books, or those best preceded by blasts on the public trumpet, which are eventually received with highest honours into the palace of literature. No more curious incident of this fact is to be found than is presented by the personal history of that enchanting classic, White's *Selborne*. If ever an author hesitated and reflected, dipped his toe into the bath of publicity, and hastily withdrew it again, loitered on the brink and could not be induced to plunge, it was the Rev. Gilbert White. This man of singular genius was not to be persuaded that the town would tolerate his lucubrations. He was ready to make a present of them to any one who would father them, he allowed his life to slip by until his seventieth year was reached, before he would print them, and when they appeared, he could not find the courage to put his name on the title-page. Not one of his own titlarks or sedge-warblers could be more shy of public observation. Even the fact that his own brother was a publisher gave him no real confidence in printers' ink.

Gilbert White was already a middle-aged man when he was drawn into correspondence by Thomas Pennant, a naturalist younger than himself, who had undertaken to produce, in four volumes folio, a work on *British Zoology* for the production of which he was radically unfitted. It has been severely, but justly, pointed out that wherever Pennant rises superior, either in style or information, to his own dead level of pompous inexactitude, he is almost certainly quoting from a letter of Gilbert White's. Yet no acknowledgment of the Selborne parson is vouchsafed;

"even in the account of the harvest-mouse," says Professor Bell, "there is no mention of its discoverer." Nevertheless, so rudimentary was scientific knowledge one hundred and thirty years ago, that Pennant's pretentious book was received with acclamation. The patient man at Selborne sat and smiled, even courteously joining with mild congratulations in the rounds of applause. Fortunately Pennant did not remain his only correspondent. The Hon. Daines Barrington was a man of another stamp, not profound, indeed, but enthusiastic, a genuine lover of research, and a gentleman at heart. He quoted Gilbert White in his writings, but never without full acknowledgment. Other friends followed, and the recluse of Selbourne became the correspondent of Sir Joseph Banks, of Dr. Chandler, and of many other great ones of that day now decently forgotten.

Meanwhile, he was growing old. Any sharp winter might have cut him off, as he trudged along through the deep lanes of his rustic parish. Early in 1770 Daines Barrington, tired of seeing his friend the mere valet to so many other pompous intellects, had proposed to him to "draw up an account of the animals of Selborne." Gilbert White put the fascinating notion from him. "It is no small undertaking," he replied, "for a man unsupported and alone to begin a natural history from his own autopsia." Pennant seems to have joined in the suggestion of Barrington, for White says (in a letter, dated July 19, 1771, which did not see the light for more than a century after it was written):

"As to any publication in this way of my own, I look upon it with great diffidence, finding that I ought to have begun it twenty years ago; but if I was to attempt anything, it should be something of a Nat: history of my native parish, an ***Annus historico-naturalis***, comprising a journal of one whole year, and illustrated with large notes and observations. Such a beginning might induce more able naturalists to write the history of various districts, and might in time occasion the production of a work so much to be wished for, a full and compleat nat: history of these kingdoms."

Three years later he was still thinking of doing something, but putting off the hour of action. In 1776 he was suddenly spurred to decide by the circumstance that Barrington had written to propose a joint work on natural history. "If I publish at all," said Gilbert White to his nephew, "I shall come forth by myself." In 1780 he is still unready: "Were it not for want of a good amanuensis, I think I should make more progress." He was now sixty years of age. Eight years later he was preparing the Index, and at last, in the autumn of 1789, the volume positively made its appearance, in the maiden author's seventieth year. Few indeed, if any, among English writers of high distinction, have been content to delay so long before testing the popular estimate of their work. His book was warmly welcomed, but the delightful author survived its publication less than four years, dying in the parish which he was to make so famous. Gilbert White was, in a very peculiar sense, a man of one book.

Countless as have been the reprints of *The Natural History of Selborne*, its original form is no longer, perhaps, familiar to many readers. The first edition, which is now before me, is a very handsome quarto. Benjamin White, the publisher, who was the younger brother of Gilbert, issued most of the standard works on natural history which appeared in London during the second half of the century, and his experience enabled him to do adequate justice to *The History of Selborne*. The frontispiece is a large folding plate of the village from the Short Lythe, an ambitious summer landscape, representing the church, White's own house, and a few cottages against the broad sweep of the hangar. On a terrace in the foreground are portrait figures of three gentlemen standing, and a lady seated. Of the former, one is a clergyman, and it has often been stated that this is Gilbert White himself; erroneously, since no portrait of him was ever executed;[1] the figure is that of the Rev. Robert Yalden, vicar of Newton-Valence. The frontispiece is unsigned, and I find no record of the artist's name. It is not to be doubted, however, that the original was painted by Samuel Hieronymus Grimm, the Swiss water-colour draughtsman, who sketched so many topographical views in the South of England.

[Note 1: That discovered in 1913 has yet to prove that it represents Gilbert White in any way.]

The remaining illustrations to this first edition, are an oval landscape vignette on the title-page, engraved by Daniel Lerpiniere; a full-page plate of some fossil shells; an extra-sized plate of the *himantopus* that was shot at Frensham Pond, straddling with an immense excess of shank; and four engravings, now of remarkable interest, displaying the village as it then stood, from various points of view. They are engraved by Peter Mazell, after drawings of Grimm's, and give what is evidently a most accurate impression of what Selborne was a century ago. In these days of reproductions, it is rather strange that no publisher has issued facsimiles of these beautiful illustrations to the original edition of what has become one of the most popular English works. For the use of book-collectors, I may go on to say that any one who is offered a copy of the edition of *The History of Selborne* of 1789, should be careful to see that not merely the plates I have mentioned are in their places, but that the engraved sub-title, with a print of the seal of Selborne Priory, occurs opposite the blank leaf which answers to page 306.

It is impossible for a bibliographer who writes on Gilbert White to resist the pleasure of mentioning the name of his best editor and biographer. It was unfortunate that Thomas Bell, who was born eight months before the death of Gilbert White, and who, quite early in life began to entertain an enthusiastic reverence for that writer, did not find an opportunity of studying Selborne on the spot until the memories of White were becoming very vague and scattered there. I think it was not until about 1865 that, retiring from a professional career, he made Selborne--and the Wakes, the very house of Gilbert White--his residence. Here he lived, however, for fifteen years, and here it was his delight to follow up every vestige of the great naturalist's sojourn in the parish. White became the passion of Professor Bell's existence, and I well recollect him when he was eighty-five or eighty-six years of age, and no longer strong enough in body to quit his room with ease, sitting in his arm-chair at the bedroom window, and directing my attention to points of Whiteish interest, as I stood in the garden below. It was as difficult for Mr. Bell to conceive that his annotations of White were complete, as it had been for White himself to pluck up courage to publish; and it was not until 1877, when the author was eighty-five years of age, that his great and final edition in two thick volumes was issued. He lived, however, to be nearly ninety, and died in the Wakes at last, in the very room, and if I mistake not, the very spot in the room, where his idol had passed away in 1793.

As long as Professor Bell was alive the house preserved, in all essentials, the identical character which it had maintained under its famous tenant. Overgrown with creepers to the very chimneys, divided by the greenest and most velvety of lawns from a many-coloured furnace of flower-beds, scarcely parted by lush paddocks from the intense green wall of the coppiced hill, the Wakes has always retained for my memory an impression of rural fecundity and summer glow absolutely unequalled. The garden seemed to burn like a green sun, with crimson stars and orange meteors to relieve it. All, I believe, has since then been altered. Selborne, they tell me, has ceased to bear any resemblance to that rich nest in which Thomas Bell so piously guarded the idea of Gilbert White. If it be so, we must live content with

The memory of what has been,
And never more may be.

THE DIARY OF A LOVER OF LITERATURE

EXTRACTS FROM THE DIARY OF A LOVER OF LITERATURE. *Ipswich: Printed and sold by John Raw; sold also by Longman, Hurst, Rees, and Orme, Paternoster Row, London*. 1810.

It may be that, save by a few elderly people and certain lovers of old *Gentleman's Magazines*, the broad anonymous quarto known as *The Diary of a Lover of Literature* is no longer much admired or even recollected. But it deserves to be recalled to memory, if only in that it was, in some respects, the first, and in others, the last of a long series of publications. It was the first of those diaries of personal record of the intellectual life, which have become more and more the fashion and have culminated at length in the ultra-refinement of Amiel and the conscious self-analysis of Marie Bashkirtseff. It was less definitely, perhaps, the last, or one of the last, expressions of the eighteenth century sentiment, undiluted by any tincture of romance, any suspicion that fine literature existed before Dryden, or could take any form unknown to Burke.

It was under a strict incognito that *The Diary of a Lover of Literature* appeared, and it was attributed by conjecture to various famous people. The real author, however, was not a celebrated man. His name was Thomas Green, and he was the grandson of a wealthy Suffolk soap-boiler, who had made a fortune during the reign of Queen Anne. The Diarist's father had been an agreeable amateur in letters, a pamphleteer, and a champion of the Church of England against Dissent. Thomas Green, who was born in 1769, found himself at twenty-five in possession of the ample family estates, a library of good books, a vast amount of leisure, and a hereditary faculty for reading. His health was not very solid, and he was debarred by it from sharing the pleasures of his neighbour squires. He determined to make books and music the occupation of his life, and in 1796, on his twenty-seventh birthday, he began to record in a diary his impressions of what he read. He went on very quietly and luxuriantly, living among his books in his house at Ipswich, and occasionally rolling in his post-chaise to valetudinarian baths and "Spaws."

When he had kept his diary for fourteen years, it seemed to a pardonable vanity so amusing, that he persuaded himself to give part of it to the world. The experiment, no doubt, was a very dubious one. After much hesitation, and in an evil hour, perhaps, he wrote: "I am induced to submit to the indulgence of the public the idlest work, probably, that ever was composed; but, I could wish to hope, not absolutely the most unentertaining or unprofitable." The welcome his volume received must speedily have reassured him, but he had pledged himself to print no more, and he kept his promise, though he went on writing his Diary until he died in 1825. His MSS. passed into the hands of John Mitford, who amused the readers of *The Gentleman's Magazine* with fragments of them for several years. Green has had many admirers in the past, amongst whom Edward FitzGerald was not the least distinguished. But he was always something of a local worthy, author of one anonymous book, and of late he has been little mentioned outside the confines of Suffolk.

It would be difficult to find an example more striking than the *Diary of a Lover of Literature* of exclusive absorption in the world of books. It opens in a gloomy year for British politics, but there is found no allusion to current events. There is a victory off Cape St. Vincent in February, 1797, but Green is attacking Bentley's annotations on Horace. Bonaparte and his army are buried in the sands of Egypt; our Diarist takes occasion to be buried in Shaftesbury's *Enquiry Concerning Virtue*. Europe rings with Hohenlinden, but the news does not reach Mr. Thomas Green, nor disturb him in his perusal of Soame Jenyns' *View of Christianity*. The fragment of the *Diary* here preserved runs from September 1796 to June 1800. No one would guess, from any word between cover and cover, that these were not halcyon years, an epoch of complete European tranquillity. War upon war might wake the echoes, but the river ran softly by the Ipswich garden of this gentle enthusiast, and not a murmur reached him through his lilacs and laburnums.

I have said that this book is one of the latest expressions of unadulterated eighteenth-century sentiment. For form's sake, the Diarist mentions now and again, very superficially, Shakespeare, Bacon, and Milton; but in reality, the garden of his study is bounded by a thick hedge behind the statue of Dryden. The classics of Greece and Rome, and the limpid reasonable writers of England from the Restoration downwards, these are enough for him. Writing in 1800 he has no suspicion of a new age preparing. We read these stately pages, and we rub our eyes. Can it be that when all this was written, Wordsworth and Coleridge had issued *Lyrical Ballads*, and Keats himself was in the world? Almost the only touch which shows consciousness of a suspicion that romantic literature existed, is a reference to the rival translations of Burger's *Lenore* in 1797. Sir Walter Scott, as we know, was one of the anonymous translators; it was, however, in all probability not his, but Taylor's, that Green mentions with special approbation.

In one hundred years a mighty change has come over the tastes and fashions of literary life. When *The Diary of a Lover of Literature* was written, Dr. Hurd, the pompous and dictatorial Bishop of Worcester, was a dreaded martinet of letters, carrying on the tradition of his yet more formidable master Warburton. As people nowadays discuss Verlaine and Ibsen, so they argued in those days about Godwin and Horne Tooke, and shuddered over each fresh incarnation of Mrs. Radcliffe. Soame Jenyns was dead, indeed, in the flesh, but his influence stalked at nights under the lamps and where disputants were gathered together in country rectories. Dr. Parr affected the Olympian nod, and crowned or checkmated reputations. "A flattering message from Dr. P----" sends our Diarist into ecstasies so excessive that a reaction sets in, and the "predominant and final effect upon my mind has been depression rather than elevation." We think of

The yarns Jack Hall invented, and the songs Jem Roper sung.   Andwhere are now Jem Roper and Jack Hall?

Who cares now for Parr's praise or Soame Jenyns' censure? Yet in our Diarist's pages these take equal rank with names that time has spared, with Robertson and Gibbon, Burke and Reynolds.

Thomas Green was more ready for experiment in art than in literature. He was "particularly struck" at the Royal Academy of 1797 with a sea view by a painter called Turner:

"Fishing vessels coming in with a heavy swell in apprehension of a tempest, gathering in the distance, and casting as it advances a night of shade, while a parting glow is spread with fine effect upon the shore; the whole composition bold in design and masterly in execution. I am entirely unacquainted with the artist, but if he proceeds as he has begun, he cannot fail to become the first in his department."

A remarkable prophecy, and one of the earliest notices we possess of the effect which the youthful Turner, then but twenty-two years of age, made on his contemporaries.

As a rule, except when he is travelling, our Diarist almost entirely occupies himself with a discussion of the books he happens to be reading. His opinions are not always in concert with the current judgment of to-day; he admires Warburton much more than we do, and Fielding much less. But he never fails to be amusing, because so independent within the restricted bounds of his intellectual domain. He is shut up in his eighteenth century like a prisoner, but inside its wall his liberty of action is complete. Sometimes his judgments are sensibly in advance of his age. It was the fashion in 1798 to denounce the Letters of Lord Chesterfield as frivolous and immoral. Green takes a wider view, and in a thoughtful analysis points out their judicious merits and their genuine parental assiduity. When Green can for a moment lift his eyes from his books, he shows a sensitive quality of observation which might have been cultivated to general advantage. Here is a reflection which seems to be as novel as it is happy:

"Looked afterwards into the Roman Catholic Chapel in Duke Street. The thrilling tinkle of the little bell at the elevation of the Host is perhaps the finest example that can be given of the sublime by association--nothing so poor and trivial in itself, nothing so transcendently awful, as indicating the sudden change in the consecrated Elements, and the instant presence of the Redeemer."

Much of the latter part of the *Diary*, as we hold it, is occupied with the description of a tour in England and Wales. Here Green is lucid, graceful, and refined: producing one after another little vignettes in prose, which remind us of the simple drawings of the water-colour masters of the age, of Girtin or Cozens or Glover. The volume, which opened with some remarks on Sir William Temple, closes with a disquisition on Warton's criticism of the poets. The curtain rises for three years on a smooth stream of intellectual reflection, unruffled by outward incident, and then falls again before we are weary of the monotonous flow of undiluted criticism. *The*

Diary of a Lover of Literature is at once the pleasing record of a cultivated mind, and a monument to a species of existence that is as obsolete as nankeen breeches or a tie-wig.

Isaac D'Israeli said that Green had humbled all modern authors to the dust, and that he earnestly wished for a dozen volumes of *The Diary*. At Green's death material for at least so many supplements were placed in the hands of John Mitford, who did not venture to produce them. From January 1834 to May 1843, however, Mitford was incessantly contributing to *The Gentleman's Magazine* unpublished extracts from this larger *Diary*. These have never been collected, but my friend, Mr. W. Aldis Wright, possesses a very interesting volume, into which the whole mass of them has been carefully and consecutively pasted, with copious illustrative matter, by the hand of Edward FitzGerald, whose interest in and curiosity about Thomas Green were unflagging.

PETER BELL AND HIS TORMENTORS

PETER BELL: *A Tale in Verse, by William Wordsworth. London: Printed by Strahan and Spottiswoode, Printers-Street: for Longman, Hurst, Rees, Orme and Brown, Paternoster Row*. 1819.

None of Wordsworth's productions are better known by name than *Peter Bell*, and yet few, probably, are less familiar, even to convinced Wordsworthians. The poet's biographers and critics have commonly shirked the responsibility of discussing this poem, and when the Primrose stanza has been quoted, and the Parlour stanza smiled at, there is usually no more said about *Peter Bell*. A puzzling obscurity hangs around its history. We have no positive knowledge why its publication was so long delayed; nor, having been delayed, why it was at length determined upon. Yet a knowledge of this poem is not merely an important, but, to a thoughtful critic, an essential element in the comprehension of Wordsworth's poetry. No one who examines that body of literature with sympathetic attention should be content to overlook the piece in which Wordsworth's theories are pushed to their furthest extremity.

When *Peter Bell* was published in April 1819, the author remarked that it had "nearly survived its *minority*; for it saw the light in the summer of 1798." It was therefore composed at Alfoxden, that plain stone house in West Somersetshire, which Dorothy and William Wordsworth rented for the sum of L23 for one year, the rent covering the use of "a large park, with seventy head of deer."

Thanks partly to its remoteness from a railway, and partly also to the peculiarities of its family history, Alfoxden remains singularly unaltered. The lover of Wordsworth who follows its deep umbrageous drive to the point where the house, the park around it, and the Quantocks above them suddenly break upon the view, sees to-day very much what Wordsworth's visitors saw when they trudged up from Stowey to commune with him in 1797. The barrier of ancient beech-trees running up into the moor, Kilve twinkling below, the stretch of fields and woods descending northward to the expanse of the yellow Severn Channel, the plain white facade of Alfoxden itself, with its easy right of way across the fantastic garden, the tumultuous pathway down to the glen, the poet's favourite parlour at the end of the house--all this presents an impression which is probably less transformed, remains more absolutely intact, than any other which can be identified with the early or even the middle life of the poet. That William and Dorothy, in their poverty, should have rented so noble a country property seems at first sight inexplicable, and the contrast between Alfoxden and Coleridge's squalid pot-house in Nether Stowey can never cease to be astonishing. But the sole object of the trustees in admitting Wordsworth to Alfoxden was, as Mrs. Sandford has discovered, "to keep the house inhabited during the minority of the owner;" it was let to the poet on the 14th of July 1797.

It was in this delicious place, under the shadow of "smooth Quantock's airy ridge," that Wordsworth's genius came of age. It was during the twelve months spent here that Wordsworth lost the final traces of the old traditional accent of poetry. It was here that the best of the *Lyrical Ballads* were written, and from this house the first volume of that epoch-making collection was forwarded to the press. Among the poems written at Alfoxden *Peter Bell* was prominent, but we hear little of it except from Hazlitt, who, taken over to the Wordsworths by Coleridge from Nether Stowey, was on a first visit permitted to read "the sibylline leaves," and on a second had the rare pleasure of hearing Wordsworth himself chant *Peter Bell*, in his "equable, sustained, and internal" manner of recitation, under the ash-trees of Alfoxden Park. I do not know whether it has been noted that the landscape of *Pe-*

ter Bell, although localised in Yorkshire by the banks of the River Swale, is yet pure Somerset in character. The poem was composed, without a doubt, as the poet tramped the grassy heights of the Quantock Hills, or descended at headlong pace, mouthing and murmuring as he went, into one sylvan combe after another. To give it its proper place among the writings of the school, we must remember that it belongs to the same group as *Tintern Abbey* and *The Ancient Mariner*.

Why, then, was it not issued to the world with these? Why was it locked up in the poet's desk for twenty-one years, and shown during that time, as we gather from its author's language to Southey, to few, even of his close friends? To these questions we find no reply vouchsafed, but perhaps it is not difficult to discover one. Every revolutionist in literature or art produces some composition in which he goes further than in any other in his defiance of recognised rules and conventions. It was Wordsworth's central theory that no subject can be too simple and no treatment too naked for poetic purposes. His poems written at Alfoxden are precisely those in which he is most audacious in carrying out his principle, and nothing, even of his, is quite so simple or quite so naked as *Peter Bell*.

Hazlitt, a very young man, strongly prejudiced in favour of the new ideas, has given us a notion of the amazement with which he listened to these pieces of Wordsworth, although he was "not critically nor sceptically inclined." Others, we know, were deeply scandalised. I have little doubt that Wordsworth himself considered that, in 1798, his own admirers were scarcely ripe for the publication of *Peter Bell*, while, even so late as June 1812, when Crabb Robinson borrowed the MS. and lent it to Charles Lamb, the latter "found nothing good in it." Robinson seems to have been the one admirer of *Peter Bell* at that time, and he was irritated at Lamb's indifference. Yet his own opinion became modified when the poem was published, and (May 3, 1819) he calls it "this *unfortunate* book."[1] In another place (June 12, 1820) Crabb Robinson says that he implored Wordsworth, before the book was printed, to omit "the party in a parlour," and also the banging of the ass's bones, but, of course, in vain.

[Note 1: The word *unfortunate* is omitted by the editor, Thomas Sadler, perhaps in deference to the feelings of Wordsworth's descendants.]

In 1819 much was changed. The poet was now in his fiftieth year. The epoch of his true productiveness was closed; all his best works, except *The Prelude*, were before the public, and although Wordsworth was by no means widely or generally recognised yet as a great poet, there was a considerable audience ready to receive with respect whatever so interesting a person should put forward. Moreover, a new generation had come to the front; Scott's series of verse-romances was closed; Byron was in mid-career; there were young men of extraordinary and somewhat disquieting talent--Shelley, Keats, and Leigh Hunt--all of whom were supposed to be, although characters of a very reprehensible and even alarming class, yet distinctly respectful in their attitude towards Mr. Wordsworth. It seemed safe to publish *Peter Bell*.

Accordingly, the thin octavo described at the head of this chapter duly appeared in April 1819. It was so tiny that it had to be eked out with the Sonnets written to W. Westall's Views, and it was adorned by an engraving of Bromley's, after a drawing specially made by Sir George Beaumont to illustrate the poem. A letter to Beaumont, unfortunately without a date, in which this frontispiece is discussed, seems to suggest that the engraving was a gift from the artist to the poet; Wordsworth, "in sorrow for the sickly taste of the public in verse," opining that he cannot afford the expense of such a frontispiece as Sir George Beaumont suggests. In accordance with these fears, no doubt, an edition of only 500 was published; but it achieved a success which Wordsworth had neither anticipated nor desired. There was a general guffaw of laughter, and all the copies were immediately sold; within a month a ribald public received a third edition, only to discover, with disappointment, that the funniest lines were omitted.

No one admired *Peter Bell*. The inner circle was silent. Baron Field wrote on the title-page of his copy, which now belongs to Mr. J. Dykes Campbell, "And his carcass was cast in the way, and the Ass stood by it." Sir Walter Scott openly lamented that Wordsworth should exhibit himself "crawling on all fours, when God has given him so noble a countenance to lift to heaven." Byron mocked aloud, and, worse than all, the young men from whom so much had been expected, *les jeunes feroces*, leaped on the poor uncomplaining Ass like so many hunting-leopards. The air was darkened by hurtling parodies, the arrangement of which is still a standing *crux* to the bibliographers.

It was Keats's friend, John Hamilton Reynolds, who opened the attack. His parody (Peter Bell: a Lyrical Ballad. London, Taylor and Hessey, 1819) was positively in the field before the original. It was said, at the time, that Wordsworth, feverishly awaiting a specimen copy of his own *Peter Bell* from town, seized a packet which the mail brought him, only to find that it was the spurious poem which had anticipated Simon Pure. *The Times* protested that the two poems must be from the same pen. Reynolds had probably glanced at proofs of the genuine poem; his preface is a close imitation of Wordsworth's introduction, and the stanzaic form in which the two pieces are written is identical. On the other hand, the main parody is made up of allusions to previous poems by Wordsworth, and shows no acquaintance with the story of *Peter Bell*. Reynolds's whole pamphlet--preface, text, and notes--is excessively clever, and touches up the bard at a score of tender points. It catches the sententious tone of Wordsworth deliciously, and it closes with this charming stanza:

> He quits that moonlight yard of skulls,
> And still he feels right glad, and smiles
> With moral joy at that old tomb;
> Peter's cheek recalls its bloom,
> And as he creepeth by the tiles,
> He mutters ever--"W.W.
> Never more will trouble you, trouble you."

Peter Bell the Second, as it is convenient, though not strictly accurate, to call Reynold's "antenatal Peter," was more popular than the original. By May a third edition had been called for, and this contained fresh stanzas and additional notes.

Another parody, which ridiculed the affection for donkeys displayed both by Wordsworth and Coleridge, was called *The Dead Asses: A Lyrical Ballad*; and an elaborate production, the author of which I have not been able to discover, was published later on in the year, *Benjamin the Waggoner* (Baldwin, Craddock and Joy, 1819), which, although the title suggests *The Waggoner* of Wordsworth, is entirely taken up with making fun of *Peter Bell*. This parody--and it is certainly neither pointless nor unskilful--chiefly deals with the poet's fantastic prologue. Then, no less a person than Shelley, writing to Leigh Hunt from Florence in November of the same year, enclosed a *Peter Bell the Third* which he desired should be printed, yet in such a form as to conceal the name of the author. Perhaps Hunt thought it indiscreet to publish this not very amusing skit, and it did not see the light till long after Shelley's death. Finally, as though the very spirit of parody danced in the company of this strange poem, Wordsworth himself chronicled its ill-fate in a sonnet imitated from Milton's defence of "Tetrachordon," singing how, on the appearance of *Peter Bell*,

> a harpy brood On Bard and Hero clamourously fell.

Of the poem which enjoyed so singular a fate, Lord Houghton has quietly remarked that it could not have been written by a man with a strong sense of humour. This is true of every part of it, of the stiff and self-sufficient preface, and of the grotesque prologue, both of which in all probability belong to 1819, no less than of the story itself, in its three cantos or parts, which bear the stamp of Alfoxden and 1798. The tale is not less improbable than uninteresting. In the first part, a very wicked potter or itinerant seller of pots, Peter Bell, being lost in the woodland, comes to the borders of a river, and thinks to steal an ass which he finds pensively hanging its head over the water; Peter Bell presently discovers that the dead body of the master of the ass is floating in the river just below. (The poet, as he has naively recorded, read this incident in a newspaper.) In the second part Peter drags the dead man to land, and starts on the ass's back to find the survivors. In the third part a vague spiritual chastisement falls on Peter Bell for his previous wickedness. Plot there is no more than this, and if proof were wanted of the inherent innocence of Wordsworth's mind, it is afforded by the artless struggles which he makes to paint a very wicked man. Peter Bell has had twelve wives, he is indifferent to primroses upon a river's brim, and he beats asses when they refuse to stir. This is really all the evidence brought against one who is described, vaguely, as combining all vices that "the cruel city breeds."

That which close students of the genius of Wordsworth will always turn to seek in *Peter Bell* is the sincere sentiment of nature and the studied simplicity of language which inspire its best stanzas. The narrative is clumsy in the extreme, and the attempts at wit and sarcasm ludicrous. Yet *Peter Bell* contains exquisite things. The Primrose stanza is known to every one; this is not so familiar:

> The dragon's wing, the magic ring,

I shall not covet for my dower.
If I along that lowly way
With sympathetic heart may stray
And with a soul of power.

Nor this, with its excruciating simplicity, its descriptive accent of 1798:

 I see a blooming Wood-boy there,
And, if I had the power to say
How sorrowful the wanderer is,
Your heart would be as sad as his
Till you had kiss'd his tears away!
 Holding a hawthorn branch in hand,
All bright with berries ripe and red;
Into the cavern's mouth he peeps--
Thence back into the moonlight creeps;
What seeks the boy?--the silent dead!

It is when he wishes to describe how Peter Bell became aware of the dead body floating under the nose of the patient ass that Wordsworth loses himself in uncouth similes. Peter thinks it is the moon, then the reflection of a cloud, then a gallows, a coffin, a shroud, a stone idol, a ring of fairies, a fiend. Last of all the poet makes the Potter, who is gazing at the corpse, exclaim:

 Is it a party in a parlour?
Cramm'd just as they on earth were cramm'd--
Some sipping punch, some sipping tea,
But, as you by their faces see,
All silent and all damned!

So deplorable is the waggishness of a person, however gifted, who has no sense of humour! This simile was too much for the gravity even of intimate friends like Southey and Lamb, and after the second edition it disappeared.

THE FANCY

THE FANCY: *A Selection from the Poetical Remains of the late Peter Cor-*

coran, of Gray's Inn, student at law. With a brief Memoir of his life. London: printed for Taylor & Hessey, Fleet Street. 1820.

The themes of the poets run in a very narrow channel. Since the old heroic times when the Homers and the Gunnlaugs sang of battle with the sleet of lances hurtling around them, a great calm has settled down upon Parnassus. Generation after generation pipes the same tune of love and Nature, of the liberal arts and the illiberal philosophies; the same imagery, the same metres, meander within the same polite margins of conventional subject. Ever and anon some one attempts to break out of the groove. In the eighteenth century they made a valiant effort to sing of The Art of Preserving Health, and of The Fleece and of The Sugar-Cane, but the innovators lie stranded, like cumbrous whales, on the shore of the ocean of Poesy. Flaubert's friend, Louis Bouilhet, made a inartful attempt to tune the stubborn lyre to music of the birthday of the world, to battles of the ichthyosaurus and the plesio-saurus, to loves of the mammoth and the mastodon. But the public would have none of it, though ensphered in faultless verso, and the poets fled back to their flames and darts, and to the primrose at the river's brim. There is, however, something pathetic, and something that pleasantly reminds us of the elasticity of the human intellect in these failures; and the book before us is an amusing example of such ec-centric efforts to enlarge the sphere of the poetic activity.

This little volume is called *The Fancy*, and it does not appear to me certain that the virtuous American conscience know what that means. If the young ladies from Wells or Wellesley inquire ingenuously, "Tell us where is Fancy bred?" we should have to reply, with a jingle, In the fists, not in the head. The poet himself, in a fit of unusual candour, says:

Fancy's a term for every blackguardism,

though this is much too severe. But rats, and they who catch them, badgers, and they who bait them, cocks, and they who fight them, and, above all, men with fists, who professionally box with them, come under the category of the *Fancy*. This, then, is the theme which the poet before us, living under the genial sway of the First Gentleman of Europe, undertook to place beneath the special patronage of Apollo. The attractions, however, of *The Learned Ring*, set all other pleasures in the shade, and the name, Peter Corcoran, which is a pseudonym, is, I suppose, chosen merely because the initials are those of the then famous Pugilistic Club. The poet is, in short, the laureate of the P.C., and his book stands in the same relation to *Boxiana* that Campbell's lyrics do to Nelson's despatches. To understand the poet's position, we ought to be dressed as he was; we ought

> to wear a tough drab coat
> With large pearl buttons all afloat
> Upon the waves of plush; to tie
> A kerchief of the king-cup die
> (White-spotted with a small bird's eye)
> Around the neck,--and from the nape
> Let fall an easy> fan-like cape,

and, in fact, to belong to that incredible company of Corinthian Tom and Jerry Hawthorn over whom Thackeray let fall so delightfully the elegiac tear.

Anthologies are not edited in a truly catholic spirit, or they would contain this very remarkable sonnet:

ON THE NONPAREIL.

> "None but himself can be his parallel."
>   With marble-coloured shoulders,--and keen eyes,
> Protected by a forehead broad and white--
> And hair cut close lest it impede the sight,
> And clenched hands, firm, and of punishing size,--
> Steadily held, or motion'd wary-wise
> To hit or stop,--and kerchief too drawn tight
> O'er the unyielding loins, to keep from flight
> The inconstant wind, that all too often flies,--
> The Nonpareil stands! Fame, whose bright eyes run o'er
> With joy to see a Chicken of her own.
> Dips her rich pen in *claret*, <and writes down
> Under the letter R, first on the score,
> "Randall,--John,--Irish Parents,--age not known,--
> Good with both hands, and only ten stone four!"

Be not too hard on this piece of barbarism, virtuous reader! Virtue is well revenged by the inevitable question! "Who was John Randall?" In 1820 it was said:

"Of all the great men in this age, in poetry, philosophy, or pugilism, there is no one of such transcendent talent as Randall, no one who combines the finest natural powers with the most elegant and finished acquired ones." Now, if his memory be revived for a moment, this master of science, who doubled up an opponent as if he were plucking a flower, and whose presence turned Moulsey Hurst into an Olympia, is in danger of being confounded with the last couple of drunken Irishwomen who have torn out each other's hair in handfuls in some Whitechapel courtyard. The mighty have fallen, the stakes and ring are gone forever, and Virtue is avenged. The days of George IV. are so long, long gone past that a paradoxical creature may be forgiven for a sigh over the ashes of the glory of John Randall.

It is strange how much genuine poetry lingers in this odd collection of verses in praise of prizefighting. There are lines and phrases that recall Keats himself, though truly the tone of the book is robust enough to satisfy the most impassioned of Tory editors. As it happens, it was written by Keats's dearest friend, by John Hamilton Reynolds, whom the great poet mentions so affectionately in the latest of all his letters. Reynolds has been treated with scant consideration by the critics. His verses, I protest, are no whit less graceful or sparkling than those of his more eminent companions, Leigh Hunt and Barry Cornwall. His **Garden of Florence** is worthy of the friend of Keats. We have seen how his **Peter Bell**, which was Peter Bell the First, took the wind out of Shelley's satiric sails and fluttered the dove-cotes of the Lakeists. He was as smart as he could be, too clever to live, in fact, too light a weight for a grave age. In **The Fancy**, which Keats seems to refer to in a letter dated January 13th, 1820, Reynolds appears to have been inspired by Tom Moore's **Tom Crib**, but if so, he vastly improves on that rather vulgar original. He takes as his motto, with adroit impertinence, some lines of Wordsworth, and persuades us

> nor need we blame the licensed joys,
> Though false to Nature's quiet equipoise:
> Frank are the sports, the stains are fugitive.

We can fancy the countenance of the Cumbrian sage at seeing his words thus nimbly adapted to be an apology for prize-fighting.

The poems are feigned to be the remains of one Peter Corcoran, student at law. A simple and pathetic memoir--which deserved to be as successful as that most felicitous of all such hoaxes, the life of the supposed Italian poet, Lorenzo Stecchetti--introduces us to the unfortunate young Irishman, who was innocently engaged to a charming lady, when, on a certain August afternoon, he strayed by chance into the Fives Court, witnessed a "sparring-exhibition" by two celebrated pugilists, and was thenceforth a lost character. From that moment nothing interested him except a favourite hit or a scientific parry, and his only topic of conversation became the noble art of self-defence. To his disgusted lady-love he took to writing eulogies of the Chicken and the Nonpareil. On one occasion he appeared before her with two black eyes, for he could not resist the temptation of taking part in the boxing, and "it is known that he has parried the difficult and ravaging hand of Randall himself." The attachment of the young lady had long been declining, and she took this opportunity of forbidding him her presence for the future. He felt this abandonment bitterly, but could not surrender the all-absorbing passion which was destroying him. He fell into a decline, and at last died "without a struggle, just after writing a sonnet to **West-Country Dick**."

The poems so ingeniously introduced consist of a kind of sporting opera called **King Tims the First**, which is the tragedy of an emigrant butcher; an epic fragment in **ottava rima**, called **The Fields of Tothill**, in which the author rambles on in the Byronic manner, and ceases, fatigued with his task, before he has begun to get his story under weigh; and miscellaneous pieces. Some of these latter are simply lyrical exercises, and must have been written in Peter Corcoran's earlier days. The most characteristic and the best deal, however, with the science of fisticuffs. Here are the lines sent by the poet to his mistress on the painful occasion which we have described above, "after a casual turn up":

Forgive me,--and never, oh, never again,
I'll cultivate light blue or brown inebriety;[1]
I'll give up all chance of a fracture or sprain,
And part, worst of all, with Pierce Egan's[2] society.
Forgive me,--and mufflers I'll carefully pull
O'er my knuckles hereafter, to make them, well-bred;
To mollify digs in the kidneys with wool,
And temper with leather a punch of the head.
And, Kate!--if you'll fib from your forehead that frown,

And spar with a lighter and prettier tone;--

I'll look,--if the swelling should ever go down,

And these eyes look again,--upon you, love, alone!

[Note 1: "Heavy **brown** with a dash of **blue** in it" was the fancy phrase for stout mixed with gin.]

[Note 2: The author of **Boxiana** and **Life in London**.]

It must be confessed that a less "fancy" vocabulary would here have shown a juster sense of Peter's position. Sometimes there is no burlesque intention apparent, but, in their curious way, the verses seem to express a genuine enthusiasm. It is neither to be expected nor to be feared that any one nowadays will seriously attempt to advocate the most barbarous of pastimes, and therefore, without conscientious scruples, we may venture to admit that these are very fine and very thrilling verses in their own unexampled class:

Oh, it is life! to see a proud

And dauntless man step, full of hopes,

Up to the P.C. stakes and ropes,

Throw in his hat, and with a spring

Get gallantly within the ring;

Eye the wide crowd, and walk awhile

Taking all cheerings with a smile;

To see him strip,--his well-trained form,

White, glowing, muscular, and warm,

All beautiful in conscious power,

Relaxed and quiet, till the hour;

His glossy and transparent frame,

In radiant plight to strive for fame!

To look upon the clean-shap'd limb

In silk and flannel clothed trim;--

While round the waist the kerchief tied

Makes the flesh glow in richer pride.

'Tis more than life, to watch him hold

His hand forth, tremulous yet bold,

Over his second's, and to clasp

His rival's in a quiet grasp;
To watch the noble attitude
He takes,--the crowd in breathless mood,--
And then to see, with adamant start,
The muscles set,--and the great heart
Hurl a courageous, splendid light
Into the eye,--and then--the FIGHT.

This is like a lithograph out of one of Pierce Egan's books, only much more spirited and picturesque, and displaying a far higher and more Hellenic sense of the beauty of athletics. Reynolds' little volume, however, enjoyed no success. The genuine amateurs of the prize-ring did not appreciate being celebrated in good verses, and *The Fancy* has come to be one of the rarest of literary curiosities.

ULTRA-CREPIDARIUS

ULTRA-CREPIDARIUS; *a Satire on William Gifford. By Leigh Hunt. London, 1823: printed for John Hunt, 22, Old Bond Street, and 38, Tavistock Street, Covent Garden*.

If the collector of first editions requires an instance from which to justify the faith which is in him against those who cry out that bibliography is naught, Leigh Hunt is a good example to his hand. This active and often admirable writer, during a busy professional life, issued a long series of works in prose and verse which are of every variety of commonness and scarcity, but which have never been, and probably never will be, reprinted as a whole. Yet not to possess the works of Leigh Hunt is to be ill-equipped for the minute study of literary history at the beginning of the century. The original 1816 edition of *Rimini*, for instance, is of a desperate rarity, yet not to be able to refer to it in the grotesqueness of this its earliest form is to miss a most curious proof of the crude taste of the young school out of which Shelley and Keats were to arise. The scarcest of all Leigh Hunt's poetical pamphlets, but by no means the least interesting, is that whose title stands at the head of this chapter. Of *Ultra-crepidarius*, which was "printed for John Hunt" in 1823, it is believed that not half a dozen copies are in existence, and it has never been reprinted.

It is a rarity, then, to which the most austere despisers of first editions may allow a special interest.

From internal evidence we find that ***Ultra-crepidarius; a Satire on William Gifford***, was sent to press in the summer of 1823, from Maiano, soon after the break-up of Hunt's household in Genoa, and Byron's departure for Greece. The poem is the "stick" which had been recently mentioned in the third number of the ***Liberal***:

Have I, these five years, spared the dog a stick,
Cut for his special use, and reasonably thick?

It had been written in 1818, in consequence of the famous review in the ***Quarterly*** of Keats's ***Endymion***, a fact which the biographers of Keats do not seem to have observed. Why did Hunt not immediately print it? Perhaps because to have done so would have been worse than useless in the then condition of public taste and temper. What led Hunt to break through his intention of suppressing the poem it might be difficult to discover. At all events, in the summer of 1823 he suddenly sent it home for publication; whether it was actually published is doubtful, it was probably only circulated in private to a handful of sympathetic Tory-hating friends.

Ultra-crepidarius is written in the same anapaestic measure as ***The Feast of the Poets***, but is somewhat longer. As a satire on William Gifford it possessed the disadvantage of coming too late in the day to be of any service to anybody. At the close of 1823 Gifford, in failing health, was resigning the editorial chair of the ***Quarterly***, which he had made so formidable, and was retiring into private life, to die in 1826. The poem probably explains, however, what has always seemed a little difficult to comprehend, the extreme personal bitterness with which Gifford, at the close of his career, regarded Hunt, since the slayer of the Della Cruscans was not the man to tolerate being treated as though he were a Della Cruscan himself. However narrow the circulation of ***Ultra-crepidarius*** may have been, care was no doubt taken that the editor of the ***Quarterly Review*** should receive one copy at his private address, and Leigh Hunt returned from Italy in time for that odd incident to take place at the Roxburgh sale, when Barron Field called his attention to the fact that "a little man, with a warped frame, and a countenance between the querulous and the angry, was gazing at me with all his might." Hunt tells this story in the ***Autobiography***, from which, however, he omits all allusion to his satire.

The latter opens with the statement that:

'Tis now about fifty or sixty years since

(The date of a charming old boy of a Prince)--

Mercury was in a state of rare fidget from the discovery that he had lost one of his precious winged shoes, and had in consequence dawdled away a whole week in company with Venus, not having dreamed that it was that crafty goddess herself, who, wishing for a pair of them, had sent one of Mercury's shoes down to Ashburton for a pattern. Venus confesses her peccadillo, and offers to descend to the Devonshire borough with her lover, and see what can have become of the ethereal shoe. As they reach the ground, they meet with an ill-favoured boot of leather, which acknowledges that it has ill-treated the delicate slipper of Mercury. This boot, of course, is Gifford, who had been a shoemaker's apprentice in Ashburton. Mercury curses this unsightly object, and part of his malediction may here be quoted.

I hear some one say "Murrain take him, the ape!"

And so Murrain shall, in a bookseller's shape;

An evil-eyed elf, in a down-looking flurry,

Who'd fain be a coxcomb, and calls himself Murray.

Adorn thou his door, like the sign of the Shoe,

For court-understrappers to congregate to;

For *Southey* to come, in his dearth of invention,

And eat his own words for mock-praise and a pension;

For *Croker* to lurk with his spider-like limb in,

And stock his lean bag with waylaying the women;

And Jove only knows for what creatures beside

To shelter their envy and dust-liking pride,

And feed on corruption, like bats, who at nights,

In the dark take their shuffles, which they call then flights;

Be these the court-critics and vamp a Review.

And by a poor figure, and therefore a true,

For it suits with thy nature, both shoe-like and slaughterly

Be its hue leathern, and title the Quarterly,

Much misconduct, and see that the others

Misdeem, and misconstrue, like miscreant brothers;
Misquote, and misplace, and mislead, and misstate,
Misapply, misinterpret, misreckon, misdate,
Misinform, misconjecture, misargue; in short,
Miss all that is good, that ye miss not the Court.

And finally, thou, my old soul of the tritical,
Noting, translating, high slavish, hot critical,
Quarterly-scutcheon'd, great heir to each dunce,
Be Tibbald, Cook, Arnall, and Dennis at once

At the end, Mercury dooms the ugly boot to take the semblance of a man, and the satire closes with its painful metamorphosis into Gifford. The poem is not without cleverness, but it is chiefly remarkable for a savage tone which is not, we think, repeated elsewhere throughout the writings of Hunt. The allusions to Gifford's relations, nearly half a century earlier, to that Earl Grosvenor who first rescued him from poverty, the well-deserved scorn of his intolerable sneers at Perdita Robinson's crutches:

Hate Woman, thou block in the path of fair feet;
If Fate want a hand to distress them, thine be it;
When the Great, and their flourishing vices, are mention'd
Say people "impute" 'em, and show thou art pension'd;
But meet with a Prince's old mistress discarded,
And then **let the world see how vice is rewarded**--

the indications of the satirist's acquaintance with the private life of his victim, all these must have stung the editor of the **Quarterly** to the quick, and are very little in Hunt's usual manner, though he had examples for them in Peter Pindar and others. There is a very early allusion to "Mr. Keats and Mr. Shelley," where, "calm, up above thee, they soar and they shine." This was written immediately after the review of **Endymion** in the **Quarterly**.

At the close is printed an extremely vigorous onslaught of Hazlitt's upon Gifford, which is better known than the poem which it illustrates. In itself, in its preface, and in its notes alike this very rare pamphlet presents us with a genuine curiosity of literature.

THE DUKE OF RUTLAND'S POEMS

ENGLAND'S TRUST AND OTHER POEMS. *By Lord John Manners. London: printed for J.G. & J. Rivington, St. Paul's Church Yard, and Waterloo Place, Pall Mall*. 1841.

My newspaper informed me this morning that Lord John Manners took his seat last night, in the Upper House, as the Duke of Rutland. These little romantic surprises are denied to Americans, who do not find that old friends get new names, which are very old names, in the course of a night. My Transatlantic readers will never have to grow accustomed to speak of Mr. Lowell as the Earl of Mount Auburn, and I firmly believe that Mr. Howells would consider it a chastisement to be hopelessly ennobled. But my thoughts went wanderting back at my breakfast to-day to those far-away times, the fresh memory of which was still reverberating about my childhood, when the last new Duke was an ardent and ingenuous young patriot, who never dreamed of being a peer, and who hoped to refashion his country to the harp of Amphion. So I turned, with assuredly no feeling of disrespect, to that corner of my library where the *peches de jeunesse* stand--the little books of early verses which the respectable authors of the same would destroy if they could--and I took down *England's Trust*.

Fifty years ago a group of young men, all of them fresh from Oxford and Cambridge, most of them more or less born in the purple of good families, banded themselves together to create a sort of aristocratic democracy. They called themselves "Young England," and the chronicle of them--is it not patent to all men in the pages of Disraeli's *Coningsby*? In the hero of that novel people saw a portrait of the leader of the group, the Hon. George Percy Sydney Smythe, to whom also the poems now before us, *parvus non parvae pignus amicitiae*, were dedicated in a warm inscription. The Sidonia of the story was doubtless only echoing what Smythe had laid down as a dogma when he said: "Man is only truly great when he acts from the passions, never irresistible but when he appeals to the imagination." It was the theory of Young England that the historic memory must be awakened in the lower classes;

that utilitarianism was sapping the very vitals of society, and that ballads and May-poles and quaint festivities and processions of a loyal peasantry were the proper things for politicians to encourage. It was all very young, and of course it came to nothing. But I do not know that the Primrose League is any improvement upon it, and I fancy that when the Duke of Rutland looks back across the half-century he sees something to smile at, but nothing to blush for.

One of the notions that Young England had got hold of was that famous saying of Fletcher of Saltoun's friend about making the ballads of a people. So they set themselves verse-making, and a quaint little collection of books it was that they produced, all smelling alike at this time of day, with a faint, faded perfume of the hay-stack, countrified and wild. Mr. Smythe, who presently became the seventh Viscount Strangford and one of the wittiest of Morning Chroniclers, only to die bitterly lamented before the age of forty, wrote **Historic Fancies**, Mr. Faber, then a fellow of University College, Oxford, and afterwards a leading spirit among English Catholics, published **The Cherwell Water-Lily**, in 1840, and on the heels of this discreet volume came the poems of Lord John Manners.

When **England's Trust** appeared, its author had just left Cambridge. Almost immediately afterward, it was decided that Young England ought to be represented in Parliament, where its Utopian chivalries, it was believed, needed only to be heard to prevail. Accordingly Lord John Manners presented himself, in June 1841, as one of the Conservative candidates for the borough of Newark. He was elected, and so was the other Tory candidate, a man already distinguished, and at present known to the entire world as Mr. W.E. Gladstone. On the hustings, Lord John Manners was a good deal heckled, and in particular he was teased excessively about a certain couplet in **England's Trust**. I am not going to repeat that couplet here, for after nearly half a century the Duke of Rutland has a right to be forgiven that extraordinary indiscretion. If any of my readers turn to the volume for themselves, which, of course, I have no power to prevent their doing, they will probably exclaim:

"Was it the Duke of Rutland who wrote **that?**" for if frequency of quotation is the hall-mark of popularity, his Grace must be one of the most popular of our living poets.

There is something exceedingly pathetic in this little volume. Its weakness as verse, for it certainly is weak, had nothing ignoble about it, and what is weak without being in the least base has already a negative distinction. The author hopes to be a Lovelace or a Montrose, equally ready to do his monarch service with sword or pen. The Duke of Rutland has not quite been a Montrose, but he has been something less brilliant and much more useful, a faithful servant of his country, through an upright and laborious life. The young poet of 1841, thrilled by the Tractarian enthusiasm of the moment, looked for a return of the high festivals of the Church, for a victory of faith over all its Paynim foes. "The worst evils," he writes, "from which we are now suffering, have arisen from our ignorant contempt or neglect of the rules of the Church." He was full of Newman and Pusey, of the great Oxford movement of 1837, of the wind of fervour blowing through England from the common-room of Oriel. Now all is changed past recognition, and with, perhaps, the solitary exception of Cardinal Newman, preserved in extreme old age, like some precious exotic, in his Birmingham cloister, the Duke of Rutland may look through the length and breadth of England without recovering one of those lost faces that fed the pure passion of his youth.

The hand which brought the flame from Oriel to the Cambridge scholar was that of the Rev. Frederick William Faber, and a great number of the poems in *England's Trust* are dedicated to him openly or secretly. Here is a sonnet addressed to Faber, which is very pleasant to read:

> Dear Friend! thou askest me to sing our loves,
> And sing them fain would I; but I do fear
> To mar so soft a theme; a theme that moves
> My heart unto its core. O friend most dear!
> No light request is thine; albeit it proves
> Thy gentleness and love, that do appear
> When absent thus, and in soft looks when near.
> Surely, if ever two fond hearts were, twined
> In a most holy, mystic knot, so now
> Are ours; not common are the ties that bind
> My soul to thine; a dear Apostle thou,
> I a young Neophyte that yearns to find
> The sacred truth, and stamp upon his brow
> The Cross, dread sign of his baptismal vow!

The Apostle was only twelve months older than the Neophyte, who was in his twenty-third year, but he was a somewhat better as well as stronger poet. *The Cherwell Water-Lily* is rather a rare book now, and I may perhaps be allowed to give an example of Faber's style. It is from one of many poems in which, with something borrowed too consciously from Wordsworth, who was the very Apollo of Young England, there Is yet a rendering of the beauty and mystery of Oxford, and of the delicate sylvan scenery which surrounds it, which is wholly original;

There is a well, a willow-shaded spot.
Cool in the noon-tide gleam,
With rushes nodding in the little stream,
And blue forget-me-not.
 Set in thick tufts along the bushy marge
With big bright eyes of gold;
And glorious water-plants, like fans, unfold
Their blossoms strange and large.
 That wandering boy, young Hylas, did not find
Beauties so rich and rare,
Where swallow-wort and pale-bright maiden's hair
And dog-grass richly twined.
 A sloping bank ran round it like a crown,
Whereon a purple cloud
Of dark wild hyacinths, a fairy crowd,
Had settled softly down.
 And dreamy sounds of never-ending bells
From Oxford's holy towers
Came down the stream, and went among the flowers,
And died in little swells.

These two extracts give a fair notion of the Tractarian poetry, with its purity, its idealism, its love of Nature and its unreal conception of life, Faber also wrote an *England's Trust*, before Lord John Manners published his; and in this he rejoices in the passing away of all the old sensual confidence, and in the coming of a new age of humility and spirituality. Alas! it never came! There was a roll in the wave of thought, a few beautiful shells were thrown up on the shore of literature, and then the little eddy of Tractarianism was broken and spent, and lost in the general progress of mankind. We touch with reverend pity the volumes without which we should scarcely know that Young England had ever existed, and we refuse to believe that all the enthusiasm and piety and courage of which they are the mere ashes have wholly passed away. They have become spread over a wide expanse of effort, and no one knows who has been graciously affected by them. Who shall say that some distant echo of the Cherwell harp was not sounding in the heart of Gordon when he went to his African martyrdom? It is her adventurers, whether of the pen or of the sword, that have made England what she is. But if every adventurer succeeded, where would the adventure be?

The Duke of Rutland soon repeated his first little heroic expedition into the land of verses. He published a volume of **English Ballads**; but this has not the historical interest which makes **England's Trust** a curiosity. He has written about Church Rates, and the Colonies, and the Importance of Literature to Men of Business, but never again of his reveries in Neville's Court nor of his determination to emulate the virtues of King Charles the Martyr. No matter! If all our hereditary legislators were as high-minded and single-hearted as the new Duke of Rutland, the reform of the House of Lords would scarcely be a burning question.

IONICA

IONICA. *Smith Elder & Co., 65, Cornhill*. 1858.

Good poetry seems to be almost as indestructible as diamonds. You throw it out of the window into the roar of London, it disappears in a deep brown slush, the omnibus and the growler pass over it, and by and by it turns up again somewhere uninjured, with all the pure fire lambent in its facets. No doubt thoroughly good specimens of prose do get lost, dragged down the vortex of a change of fashion, and never thrown back again to light. But the quantity of excellent verse produced in any generation is not merely limited, but keeps very fairly within the same proportions. The verse-market is never really glutted, and while popular masses of what Robert Browning calls "deciduous trash" survive their own generation, only to be carted away, the little excellent, unnoticed book gradually pushes its path up silently into fame.

These reflections are not inappropriate in dealing with the small volume of 116 pages called *Ionica*, long ago ushered into the world so silently that its publication did not cause a single ripple on the sea of literature. Gradually this book has become first a rarity and then a famous possession, so that at the present moment there is perhaps no volume of recent English verse so diminutive which commands so high a price among collectors. When the library of Mr. Henry Bradshaw was dispersed in November 1886, book-buyers thought that they had a chance of securing this treasure at a reasonable price, for it was known that the late Librarian of Cambridge University, an old friend of the author, had no fewer than three copies. But at the sale two of these copies went for three pounds fifteen and three pounds ten, respectively, and the third was knocked down for a guinea, because it was discovered to lack the title-page and the index. (I do not myself think it right to encourage the sale of imperfect books, and would not have spent half a crown on the rarest of volumes if I could not have the title-page. But this is only an aside, and does not interfere with the value of *Ionica*.)

The little book has no name on the title-page, but it is known that the author was Mr. William Johnson, formerly a master at Eton and a fellow of King's College, Cambridge. It is understood that this gentleman was born about 1823, and died in 1892. On coming into property, as I have heard, in the west of England, he took the name of Cory, So that he is doubly concealed as a poet, the anonymous-pseudonymous. As Mr. William Cory he wrote history, but there is but slight trace there of the author of *Ionica*. In face of the extreme rarity of his early book, friends urged upon Mr. Cory its republication, and he consented. Probably he would have done well to refuse, for the book is rather delicate and exquisite than forcible, and to reprint it was to draw public attention to its inequality. Perhaps I speak with the narrow-mindedness of the collector who possesses a treasure; but I think the appreciators of *Ionica* will always be few in number, and it seems good for those few to have some difficulties thrown in the way of their delights.

Shortly after *Ionica* appeared great developments took place in English verse. In 1858 there was no Rossetti, no Swinburne; we may say that, as far as the general public was concerned, there was no Matthew Arnold and no William Morris. This fact has to be taken into consideration in dealing with the tender humanism of Mr.

Johnson's verses. They are less coruscating and flamboyant than what we became accustomed to later on. The tone is extremely pensive, sensitive, and melancholy. But where the author is at his best, he is not only, as it seems to me, very original, but singularly perfect, with the perfection of a Greek carver of gems. The book is addressed to and intended for scholars, and the following piece, although really a translation, has no statement to that effect. Before I quote it, perhaps I may remind the ladies that the original is an epigram in the Greek Anthology, and that it was written by the great Alexandrian poet Callimachus on hearing the news that his dear friend, the poet Heraclitus--not to be confounded with the philosopher--was dead.

> They told me, Heraclitus, they told me you were dead;
> They brought me bitter news to hear and bitter tears to shed
> I wept, as I remembered, how often you and I
> Had tired the sun with talking and sent him down the sky.
> And now that thou art lying, my dear old Carian guest,
> A handful of grey ashes, long long ago at rest,
> Still are thy pleasant voices, thy nightingales, awake;
> For Death, he taketh all away, but these he cannot take.

No translation ever smelt less of the lamp, and more of the violet than this. It is an exquisite addition to a branch of English literature, which is already very rich, the poetry of elegiacal regret. I do not know where there is to be found a sweeter or tenderer expression of a poet's grief at the death of a poet-friend, grief mitigated only by the knowledge that the dead man's songs, his "nightingales," are outliving him. It is the requiem of friendship, the reward of one who, in Keats's wonderful phrase, has left "great verse unto a little clan," the last service for the dead to whom it was enough to be "unheard, save of the quiet primrose, and the span of heaven, and few ears." To modern vulgarity, whose ideal of Parnassus is a tap-room of howling politicians, there is nothing so offensive, as there is nothing so incredible, as the notion that a poet may hold his own comrade something dearer than the public. The author of *Ionica* would deserve well of his country if he had done no more than draw this piece of aromatic calamus-root from the Greek waters.

Among the lyrics which are entirely original, there are several not less exquisite than this memory of Callimachus. But the author is not very safe on modern ground. I confess that I shudder when I read:

"Oh, look at his jacket, I know him afar;

How nice," cry the ladies, "looks yonder Hussar!"

It needs a peculiar lightness of hand to give grace to these colloquial numbers, and the author of **Ionica** is more at home in the dryad-haunted forest with Comatas. In combining classic sentiment with purely English landscape he is wonderfully happy.

There is not a jarring image or discordant syllable to break the glassy surface of this plaintive **Dirge**:

Naiad, hid beneath the bank
By the willowy river-side,
Where Narcissus gently sank,
Where unmarried Echo died,
Unto thy serene repose
Waft the stricken Anteros.

Where the tranquil swan is borne,
Imaged in a watery glass,
Where the sprays of fresh pink thorn
Stoop to catch the boats that pass,
Where the earliest orchis grows,
Bury thou fair Anteros.

On a flickering wave we gaze,
Not upon his answering eyes:
Flower and bird we scarce can praise,
Having lost his sweet replies:
Cold and mute the river flows
With our tears for Anteros.

We know well where this place of burial is to be. Not in some glade of Attica or by Sicilian streams, but where a homelier river gushes through the swollen lock at Bray, or shaves the smooth pastoral meadows at Boveney, where Thames begins to draw a longer breath for his passage between Eton and Windsor.

The prevailing sentiment of these poems is a wistful clinging to this present life, a Pagan optimism which finds no fault with human existence save that it is so brief. It gains various expression in words that seem hot on a young man's lips, and warm on the same lips even when no longer young:

I'll borrow life, and not grow old;

And nightingales and trees

Shall keep me, though the veins be cold,

As young as Sophocles.

And again, in poignant notes:

You promise heavens free from strife,

Pure truth, and perfect change of will;

But sweet, sweet is this human life,

So sweet, I fain would breathe it still;

Your chilly stars I can forego,

This warm, kind world is all I know.

This last quotation is from the poem called ***Mimnermus in Church***. In this odd title he seems to refer to elegies of the Colophonian poet, who was famous in antiquity for the plaintive stress which he laid on the necessity of extracting from life all it had to offer, since there was nothing beyond mortal love, which was the life of life. The author of ***Ionica*** seems to bring the old Greek fatalist to modern England, and to conduct him to church upon a Sunday morning. But Mimnermus is impenitent. He confesses that the preacher is right when he says that all earthly pleasures are fugitive. He has always confessed as much at home under the olive tree; it was because they were fugitive that he clung to them:

All beauteous things for which we live

By laws of time and space decay.

But oh! the very reason why

I clasp them, is because they die.

There is perhaps no modern book of verse in which a certain melancholy phase of ancient thought is better reproduced than in ***Ionica***, and this gives its slight verses their lasting charm. We have had numerous resuscitations of ancient manners and landscape in modern poetry since the days of Keats and Andre Chenier. Many of these have been so brilliantly successful that only pedantry would deny their value. But in ***Ionica*** something is given which the others have not known how to give, the murmur of antiquity, the sigh in the grass of meadows dedicated to Perse-phone. It seems to help us to comprehend the little rites and playful superstitions of the Greeks; to see why Myro built a tomb for the grasshopper she loved and lost; why the shining hair of Lysidice, when she was drowned, should be hung up with songs of pity and reproach in the dreadful vestibule of Aphrodite. The noisy blasphemers of the newest Paris strike the reader as Christian fanatics turned inside out; for all their vehemence they can never lose the experience of their religious birth. The same thing is true of the would-be Pagans of a milder sensuous type. The Cross prevailed at their nativity, and has thrown its shadow over their conscience. But in the midst of the throng there walks this plaintive poet of the *Ionica*, the one genuine Pagan, absolutely untouched by the traditions of the Christian past. I do not commend the fact; I merely note it as giving a strange interest to these forlorn and unpopular poems.

Twenty years after the publication of *Ionica*, and when that little book had become famous among the elect, the author printed at Cambridge a second part, without a title-page, and without punctuation, one of the most eccentric looking pamphlets I ever saw. The enthusiastic amateur will probably regard his collection incomplete without *Ionica II.*, but he must be prepared for a disappointment. There is a touch of the old skill here and there, as in such stanzas as this:

With half a moon, and clouds rose-pink,
And water-lilies just in bud,
With iris on the river-brink,
And white weed-garlands on the mud,
And roses thin and pale as dreams,
And happy cygnets born in May,
No wonder if our country seems
Drest out for Freedom's natal day.
Or these:
Peace lit upon a fluttering vein,
And self-forgetting on the brain;
On rifts by passion wrought again
Splashed from the sky of childhood rain,
And rid of afterthought were we

And from foreboding sweetly free.
 Now falls the apple, bleeds the vine,
And, moved by some autumnal sign,
I who in spring was glad repine
And ache without my anodyne;
Oh! things that were! Oh! things that are!
Oh! setting of my double star!

But these are rare, and the old unique *Ionica* of thirty years earlier is not repeated.

THE SHAVING OF SHAGPAT

THE SHAVING OF SHAGPAT. *An Arabian Entertainment. By George Meredith. Chapman and Hall*. 1856.

It is nearly forty years since I first heard of *The Shaving of Shagpat*. I was
newly come, in all my callow ardour, into the covenant of Art and Letters, and I
was moving about, still bewildered, in a new world. In this new world, one afternoon, Dante Gabriel Rossetti, standing in front of his easel, remarked to all present
whom it should concern, that *The Shaving of Shagpat* was a book which Shakespeare might have been glad to write. I now understand that in the warm Rossetti-
language this did not mean that there was anything specially reminiscent of the
Bard of Avon in this book, but simply that it was a monstrous fine production, and
worthy of all attention. But at the time I expected, from such a title, something in
the way of a belated *Midsummer Night's Dream* or *Love's Labour's Lost*. I was
fully persuaded that it must be a comedy, and as the book even then was rare, and
as I was long pursuing the loan of it, I got this dramatic notion upon my mind, and
to this day do still clumsily connect it with the idea of Shakespeare. But in truth *The
Shaving of Shagpat* has no other analogy with those plays, which Bacon would
have written if he had been so plaguily occupied, than that it is excellent in quality
and of the finest literary flavour.

The ordinary small collection of rarities has no room for three-volume novels, those signs-manual of our British dulness and crafty disdain for literature. One

or two of these *simulacra*, these sham-semblances of books, I possess, because honoured friends have given them to me; even so, I would value the gift more in the decency of a single volume. The dear little duodecimos of the last century, of course, are welcome in a library. That was a happy day, when by the discovery of a *Ferdinand Count Fathom*, I completed my set of Smollett in the original fifteen volumes. But after the first generation of novelists, the sham system began to creep in. With Fanny Burney, novels grow too bulky, and it is a question whether even Scott or Jane Austen should be possessed in the original form. Of the moderns, only Thackeray is bibliographically desirable. Hence even of Mr. George Meredith's fiction I make no effort to possess first editions; yet *The Shaving of Shagpat* is an exception. I toiled long to secure it, and, now that I hold it, may its modest vermilion cover shine always like a lamp upon my shelves! It is not fiction to a bibliophile; it is worthy of all the honour done to verse.

Within the last ten years of his life we had the great pleasure of seeing tardy justice done at length to the genius of Mr. George Meredith. I like to think that, after a long and noble struggle against the inattention of the public, after the pouring of high music for two generations into ears whose owners seemed to have wilfully sealed them with wax, so that only the most staccato and least happy notes ever reached their dulness, George Meredith did, before the age of seventy, reap a little of his reward. I am told that the movement in favour of him began in America; if so, more praise to American readers, who had to teach us to appreciate De Quincey and Praed before we knew the value of those men. Yet is there much to do. Had George Meredith been a Frenchman, what monographs had ere this been called forth by his work; in Germany, or Italy, or Denmark even, such gifts as his would long ago have found their classic place above further discussion. But England is a Gallio, and in defiance of Mr. Le Gallienne, cares little for the things of literature.

If a final criticism of George Meredith existed, where in it would *The Shaving of Shagpat* find its place? There is fear that in competition with the series of analytical studies of modern life that stretches from *The Ordeal of Richard Feverel* to *One of our Conquerors*, it might chance to be pushed away with a few lines of praise. Now, I would not seem so paradoxical as to say that when an extravaganza is held up to me in one hand, and a masterpiece of morality like *The Egoist* in the other, I can doubt which is the greater book; but there are moods in which I am jealous of the novels, and wish to be left alone with my ***Arabian Entertainment***. Delicious in this harsh world of reality to fold a mist around us, and out of it to evolve the yellow domes and black cypresses, the silver fountains and marble pillars, of the fabulous city of Shagpat. I do not know any later book than ***The Shaving*** in which an Englishman has allowed his fancy, untrammelled by any sort of moral or intellectual subterfuge, to go a-roaming by the light of the moon. We do this sort of thing no longer. We are wholly given up to realism, we are harshly pressed upon on all sides by the importunities of excess of knowledge. If we talk of gryphons, the zoologists are upon us; of Oolb or Aklis, the geographers flourish their maps at us in defiance. But the author of ***The Shaving of Shagpat***, in the bloom of his happy youthful genius, defied all this pedantry. In a little address which has been suppressed in later editions he said (December 8, 1855)

"It has seemed to me that the only way to tell an Arabian Story was by imitating the style and manner of the Oriental Story-tellers. But such an attempt, whether successful or not, may read like a translation. I therefore think it better to prelude this Entertainment by an avowal that it springs from no Eastern source, and is in every respect an original Work."

If one reader of ***The Shaving of Shagpat*** were to confess the truth he would say that to him at least the other, the genuine Oriental tales, appear the imitation, and not a very good imitation. The true genius of the East breathes in Meredith's pages, and the ***Arabian Nights***, at all events in the crude literality of Sir Richard Burton, pale before them like a mirage. The variety of scenes and images, the untiring evolution of plot, the kaleidoscopic shifting of harmonious colours, all these seem of the very essence of Arabia, and to coil directly from some bottle of a genie. Ah! what a bottle! As we whirl along in the vast and glowing bacchanal, we cry, like Sganarelle:

Qu'ils sont doux--
Bouteille jolie--
Qu'ils sont doux
Vos petits glou-glous;
Ah! Bouteille, ma mie;
Pourquoi vous videz-vous?

Ah! why indeed? For ***The Shaving of Shagpat*** is one of those very rare modern books of which it is certain that they are too short, and even our excitement at the Mastery of the Event is tamed by a sense that the show is closing, and that Shibli Bagarag has been too promptly successful in smiting through the Identical. But perhaps of all gifts there is none more rare than this of clearing the board and leaving the reader still hungry.

Who shall say, in dealing with such a book, what passage in it is best or worst? Either the fancy, carried away utterly captive, follows the poet whither he will, or the whole conception is a failure. Perhaps, after the elemental splendour and storm of the final scene, what clings most to the memory is how Shibli Bagarag, hard beset in the Cave of Chrysolites, touched the great lion with the broken sapphire hair of Garraveen; or again, how on the black coast of the enchanted sea, wandering by moonlight, he found the sacred Lily, and tore it up, and lo! its bulb was a palpitating heart of human flesh; or how Bhanavar called the unwilling serpents too often, and failed to win her beauty back, till, at an awful price she once more, and for the last time, contrived to call her body-guard of snakes hissing and screaming around her.

There is surely no modern book so unsullied as this is by the modern spirit, none in which the desire to teach a lesson, to refer knowingly to topics of the day, or worst of all, to be incontinently funny, interferes less with the tender magic of Oriental fancy, or with the childlike, earnest faith in what is utterly outside the limits of experience. It belongs to that infancy of the world, when the happy guileless human being still holds that somewhere there is a flower to be plucked, a lamp to be rubbed, or a form of words to be spoken which will reverse the humdrum laws of Nature, call up unwilling spirits bound to incredible services, and change all this brown life of ours to scarlet and azure and mother-of-pearl. Little by little, even our children are losing this happy gift of believing the incredible, and that class of writing which seems to require less effort than any other, and to be a mere spinning of gold thread out of the poet's inner consciousness, is less and less at command, and when executed gives less and less satisfaction. The gnomes of Pope, the fays and "trilbys" of Nodier, even the fairy-world of Doyle, are breathed upon by a race that has grown up habituated to science. But even for such a race it must be long before the sumptuous glow and rich triumphant humour of *The Shaving of Shagpat* have lost all their attraction.

The Codes Of Hammurabi And Moses
W. W. Davies

QTY

The discovery of the Hammurabi Code is one of the greatest achievements of archaeology, and is of paramount interest, not only to the student of the Bible, but also to all those interested in ancient history...

Religion   **ISBN:** *1-59462-338-4*   **Pages:132**
MSRP $12.95

The Theory of Moral Sentiments
Adam Smith

QTY

This work from 1749. contains original theories of conscience amd moral judgment and it is the foundation for systemof morals.

Philosophy   **ISBN:** *1-59462-777-0*   **Pages:536**
MSRP $19.95

Jessica's First Prayer
Hesba Stretton

QTY

In a screened and secluded corner of one of the many railway-bridges which span the streets of London there could be seen a few years ago, from five o'clock every morning until half past eight, a tidily set-out coffee-stall, consisting of a trestle and board, upon which stood two large tin cans, with a small fire of charcoal burning under each so as to keep the coffee boiling during the early hours of the morning when the work-people were thronging into the city on their way to their daily toil...

Childrens   **ISBN:** *1-59462-373-2*   **Pages:84**
MSRP $9.95

My Life and Work
Henry Ford

QTY

Henry Ford revolutionized the world with his implementation of mass production for the Model T automobile. Gain valuable business insight into his life and work with his own auto-biography... "We have only started on our development of our country we have not as yet, with all our talk of wonderful progress, done more than scratch the surface. The progress has been wonderful enough but..."

Biographies/   **ISBN:** *1-59462-198-5*   **Pages:300**

MSRP $21.95

The Art of Cross-Examination
Francis Wellman

QTY

I presume it is the experience of every author, after his first book is published upon an important subject, to be almost overwhelmed with a wealth of ideas and illustrations which could readily have been included in his book, and which to his own mind, at least, seem to make a second edition inevitable. Such certainly was the case with me; and when the first edition had reached its sixth impression in five months, I rejoiced to learn that it seemed to my publishers that the book had met with a sufficiently favorable reception to justify a second and considerably enlarged edition. ...

Pages:412

Reference   ISBN: *1-59462-647-2*   *MSRP $19.95*

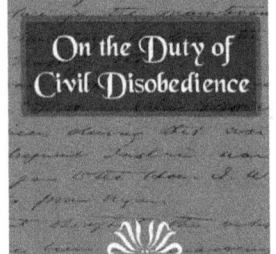

On the Duty of Civil Disobedience
Henry David Thoreau

QTY

Thoreau wrote his famous essay, On the Duty of Civil Disobedience, as a protest against an unjust but popular war and the immoral but popular institution of slave-owning. He did more than write—he declined to pay his taxes, and was hauled off to gaol in consequence. Who can say how much this refusal of his hastened the end of the war and of slavery ?

Law   ISBN: *1-59462-747-9*   **Pages:48**

MSRP $7.45

Dream Psychology
Psychoanalysis for Beginners

Sigmund Freud

Dream Psychology Psychoanalysis for Beginners
Sigmund Freud

QTY

Sigmund Freud, born Sigismund Schlomo Freud (May 6, 1856 - September 23, 1939), was a Jewish-Austrian neurologist and psychiatrist who co-founded the psychoanalytic school of psychology. Freud is best known for his theories of the unconscious mind, especially involving the mechanism of repression; his redefinition of sexual desire as mobile and directed towards a wide variety of objects; and his therapeutic techniques, especially his understanding of transference in the therapeutic relationship and the presumed value of dreams as sources of insight into unconscious desires.

Pages:196

Psychology   ISBN: *1-59462-905-6*   *MSRP $15.45*

The Miracle of Right Thought
Orison Swett Marden

QTY

Believe with all of your heart that you will do what you were made to do. When the mind has once formed the habit of holding cheerful, happy, prosperous pictures, it will not be easy to form the opposite habit. It does not matter how improbable or how far away this realization may see, or how dark the prospects may be, if we visualize them as best we can, as vividly as possible, hold tenaciously to them and vigorously struggle to attain them, they will gradually become actualized, realized in the life. But a desire, a longing without endeavor, a yearning abandoned or held indifferently will vanish without realization.

Pages:360

Self Help   ISBN: *1-59462-644-8*   *MSRP $25.45*

The Rosicrucian Cosmo-Conception Mystic Christianity *by Max Heindel*　ISBN: *1-59462-188-8*　**$38.95**
The Rosicrucian Cosmo-conception is not dogmatic, neither does it appeal to any other authority than the reason of the student. It is: not controversial, but is: sent forth in the, hope that it may help to clear...　New Age/Religion Pages 646

Abandonment To Divine Providence *by Jean-Pierre de Caussade*　ISBN: *1-59462-228-0*　**$25.95**
"The Rev. Jean Pierre de Caussade was one of the most remarkable spiritual writers of the Society of Jesus in France in the 18th Century. His death took place at Toulouse in 1751. His works have gone through many editions and have been republished...　Inspirational/Religion Pages 400

Mental Chemistry *by Charles Haanel*　ISBN: *1-59462-192-6*　**$23.95**
Mental Chemistry allows the change of material conditions by combining and appropriately utilizing the power of the mind. Much like applied chemistry creates something new and unique out of careful combinations of chemicals the mastery of mental chemistry...　New Age Pages 354

The Letters of Robert Browning and Elizabeth Barret Barrett 1845-1846 vol II　ISBN: *1-59462-193-4*　**$35.95**
by Robert Browning and Elizabeth Barrett　Biographies Pages 596

Gleanings In Genesis (volume I) *by Arthur W. Pink*　ISBN: *1-59462-130-6*　**$27.45**
Appropriately has Genesis been termed "the seed plot of the Bible" for in it we have, in germ form, almost all of the great doctrines which are afterwards fully developed in the books of Scripture which follow...　Religion/Inspirational Pages 420

The Master Key *by L. W. de Laurence*　ISBN: *1-59462-001-6*　**$30.95**
In no branch of human knowledge has there been a more lively increase of the spirit of research during the past few years than in the study of Psychology, Concentration and Mental Discipline. The requests for authentic lessons in Thought Control, Mental Discipline and...　New Age/Religion Pages 422

The Lesser Key Of Solomon Goetia *by L. W. de Laurence*　ISBN: *1-59462-092-X*　**$9.95**
This translation of the first book of the "Lernegton" which is now for the first time made accessible to students of Talismanic Magic was done, after careful collation and edition, from numerous Ancient Manuscripts in Hebrew, Latin, and French...　New Age/Occult Pages 92

Rubaiyat Of Omar Khayyam *by Edward Fitzgerald*　ISBN:*1-59462-332-5*　**$13.95**
Edward Fitzgerald, whom the world has already learned, in spite of his own efforts to remain within the shadow of anonymity, to look upon as one of the rarest poets of the century, was born at Bredfield, in Suffolk, on the 31st of March, 1809. He was the third son of John Purcell...　Music Pages 172

Ancient Law *by Henry Maine*　ISBN: *1-59462-128-4*　**$29.95**
The chief object of the following pages is to indicate some of the earliest ideas of mankind, as they are reflected in Ancient Law, and to point out the relation of those ideas to modern thought.　Religiom/History Pages 452

Far-Away Stories *by William J. Locke*　ISBN: *1-59462-129-2*　**$19.45**
"Good wine needs no bush, but a collection of mixed vintages does. And this book is just such a collection. Some of the stories I do not want to remain buried for ever in the museum files of dead magazine-numbers an author's not unpardonable vanity..."　Fiction Pages 272

Life of David Crockett *by David Crockett*　ISBN: *1-59462-250-7*　**$27.45**
"Colonel David Crockett was one of the most remarkable men of the times in which he lived. Born in humble life, but gifted with a strong will, an indomitable courage, and unremitting perseverance...　Biographies/New Age Pages 424

Lip-Reading *by Edward Nitchie*　ISBN: *1-59462-206-X*　**$25.95**
Edward B. Nitchie, founder of the New York School for the Hard of Hearing, now the Nitchie School of Lip-Reading, Inc, wrote "LIP-READING Principles and Practice". The development and perfecting of this meritorious work on lip-reading was an undertaking...　How-to Pages 400

A Handbook of Suggestive Therapeutics, Applied Hypnotism, Psychic Science　ISBN: *1-59462-214-0*　**$24.95**
by Henry Munro　Health/New Age/Health/Self-help Pages 376

A Doll's House: and Two Other Plays *by Henrik Ibsen*　ISBN: *1-59462-112-8*　**$19.95**
Henrik Ibsen created this classic when in revolutionary 1848 Rome. Introducing some striking concepts in playwriting for the realist genre, this play has been studied the world over.　Fiction/Classics/Plays 308

The Light of Asia *by sir Edwin Arnold*　ISBN: *1-59462-204-3*　**$13.95**
In this poetic masterpiece, Edwin Arnold describes the life and teachings of Buddha. The man who was to become known as Buddha to the world was born as Prince Gautama of India but he rejected the worldly riches and abandoned the reigns of power when...　Religion/History/Biographies Pages 170

The Complete Works of Guy de Maupassant *by Guy de Maupassant*　ISBN: *1-59462-157-8*　**$16.95**
"For days and days, nights and nights, I had dreamed of that first kiss which was to consecrate our engagement, and I knew not on what spot I should put my lips..."　Fiction/Classics Pages 240

The Art of Cross-Examination *by Francis L. Wellman*　ISBN: *1-59462-309-0*　**$26.95**
Written by a renowned trial lawyer, Wellman imparts his experience and uses case studies to explain how to use psychology to extract desired information through questioning.　How-to/Science/Reference Pages 408

Answered or Unanswered? *by Louisa Vaughan*　ISBN: *1-59462-248-5*　**$10.95**
Miracles of Faith in China　Religion Pages 112

The Edinburgh Lectures on Mental Science (1909) *by Thomas*　ISBN: *1-59462-008-3*　**$11.95**
This book contains the substance of a course of lectures recently given by the writer in the Queen Street Hall, Edinburgh. Its purpose is to indicate the Natural Principles governing the relation between Mental Action and Material Conditions...　New Age/Psychology Pages 148

Ayesha *by H. Rider Haggard*　ISBN: *1-59462-301-5*　**$24.95**
Verily and indeed it is the unexpected that happens! Probably if there was one person upon the earth from whom the Editor of this, and of a certain previous history, did not expect to hear again...　Classics Pages 380

Ayala's Angel *by Anthony Trollope*　ISBN: *1-59462-352-X*　**$29.95**
The two girls were both pretty, but Lucy who was twenty-one who supposed to be simple and comparatively unattractive, whereas Ayala was credited, as her Bombwhat romantic name might show, with poetic charm and a taste for romance. Ayala when her father died was nineteen...　Fiction Pages 484

The American Commonwealth *by James Bryce*　ISBN: *1-59462-286-8*　**$34.45**
An interpretation of American democratic political theory. It examines political mechanics and society from the perspective of Scotsman James Bryce　Politics Pages 572

Stories of the Pilgrims *by Margaret P. Pumphrey*　ISBN: *1-59462-116-0*　**$17.95**
This book explores pilgrims religious oppression in England as well as their escape to Holland and eventual crossing to America on the Mayflower, and their early days in New England...　History Pages 268

QTY

The Fasting Cure *by Sinclair Upton*
ISBN: *1-59462-222-1* **$13.95**

In the Cosmopolitan Magazine for May, 1910, and in the Contemporary Review (London) for April, 1910, I published an article dealing with my experiences in fasting. I have written a great many magazine articles, but never one which attracted so much attention... New Age/Self Help/Health Pages 164

Hebrew Astrology *by Sepharial*
ISBN: *1-59462-308-2* **$13.45**

In these days of advanced thinking it is a matter of common observation that we have left many of the old landmarks behind and that we are now pressing forward to greater heights and to a wider horizon than that which represented the mind-content of our progenitors... Astrology Pages 144

Thought Vibration or The Law of Attraction in the Thought World
ISBN: *1-59462-127-6* **$12.95**

by William Walker Atkinson
Psychology/Religion Pages 144

Optimism *by Helen Keller*
ISBN: *1-59462-108-X* **$15.95**

Helen Keller was blind, deaf, and mute since 19 months old, yet famously learned how to overcome these handicaps, communicate with the world, and spread her lectures promoting optimism. An inspiring read for everyone... Biographies/Inspirational Pages 84

Sara Crewe *by Frances Burnett*
ISBN: *1-59462-360-0* **$9.45**

In the first place, Miss Minchin lived in London. Her home was a large, dull, tall one, in a large, dull square, where all the houses were alike, and all the sparrows were alike, and where all the door-knockers made the same heavy sound... Childrens/Classic Pages 88

The Autobiography of Benjamin Franklin *by Benjamin Franklin*
ISBN: *1-59462-135-7* **$24.95**

The Autobiography of Benjamin Franklin has probably been more extensively read than any other American historical work, and no other book of its kind has had such ups and downs of fortune. Franklin lived for many years in England, where he was agent... Biographies/History Pages 332

Name	
Email	
Telephone	
Address	
City, State ZIP	

☐ **Credit Card**   ☐ **Check / Money Order**

Credit Card Number	
Expiration Date	
Signature	

Please Mail to: Book Jungle
PO Box 2226
Champaign, IL 61825
or Fax to: 630-214-0564